ISLANDS

ISLANDS

·GRAHAM SHEIL·

First published 1986
by Pascoe Publishing Pty Ltd
P.O. Box 51, Fairfield 3078
Australia

Islands
ISBN 0 9592104 8 2

Printed in Australia by
The Dominion Press–Hedges and Bell
Maryborough
Typeset in Palatino by Bookset

Cover art and book design by Stephen Pascoe

You cannot build bridges between the wandering islands
The Mind has no neighbours, and the unteachable heart
Announces its armistice time after time, but spends
Its love to draw them closer and closer apart.

A. D. Hope
Wandering Islands

Acknowledgements

The Bridge Pool, first published in The Brisbane Sunday Mail, *Vera*, first published in Inprint, *The Picking Season*, first published in Southerly, *Mad Like Lasseter*, first published in Westerly and performed as stage play in Adelaide and Goulburn, *The Queen Says Mix*, first published in Australian Short Stories, *Fritz*, first published in Australia Short Stories, *Mister Al*, first published by Syme Community Newspapers, *The Suppliant*, first published in Westerly, *Letter to Hans*, first published in Inprint, *Tommy Garrett's Name*, winner of Rolf Bolderwood Award for Short Stories, first published in Australian Short Stories, *Dogs in Denpassar*, first published in The Sun News-Pictorial, *Mime With Fox and Hawk*, winner of The Sun News-Pictorial Festival of Short Stories Award, first published in The Sun News-Pictorial, *The Notepad*, first published in Southerly, *Mother's Nose*, first published in Inprint, *A Burgomaster's Story*, first published in The Sun News-Pictorial.

Contents

The Queen Says Mix

They ran at the edge of the road, the sounds of their running seeming to hang in the early-morning stillness. Robby's sandshoes made soft *t-tsks t-tsks* on the roadside gravel, but Nelson's gym-boots slapped hard on bitumen. Sunlight flared on the wet bitumen where puddles expired in whisps of vapour.

They ran past the jetty, around the corner where the shops began. And there was Celestina, coming with bread from the bakery. Celestina called:

'Hey Nelson! Fight 'em Nelson! Get there — fight 'em!'

Nelson ran to the centre of the road, turned, shadow-boxed a furious set of punches toward Celestina who tossed her head back in wide gap-toothed laughter. Her dress was tight across her broad belly and so much of her breasts as were above the top of her dress were set quivering like prodded jelly-fish.

Celestina's laughter followed as they ran beneath the high eucalypts in the caravan park, to the beach. Nelson sprinted away on the hard sand at the water's edge, then shadow-boxed until Robby caught up. Nelson said:

'It's not me Wise-boy 's comin' t' see.'

Robby was looking out to sea where now the sun drew back mist at the rim of sky to reveal the long and low undulations of an island. The island was a blue deeper than the light-spangled blue of sea, deeper than the pallid blue of sky rim.

'I'm the excuse,' Nelson said.

They ran, scattering gulls that rose in raucous clamour to hover over whiting heads, backbones, tails from which the fillets had been cut.

'You go with Wise-boy,' Nelson said. 'You make money.'

'Sounds like Wise-boy's got you on percentage to talk me 'round.'

'Not me, brother. But Wise-boy lost three Australian champs in a year. He reckoned on getting one back with me — till Bettiol punched me from ropes t' canvas. He needs a good new nag for his stable.'

'Long as his stable's in Sydney he won't rope me.'

'For a whitey, Wise-boy's the best. Even fighting prelim he works the bookies so you make money. And for your mare — it'd be back to her home paddock. Just what she's been neighin' for.'

'Iris don't know Wise-boy's coming. Not yet.'

They ran from the water's edge to the high eucalypts margining the beach, then to the esplanade, running back beside the road. Now there were cars. Some drivers tooted and waved to Nelson. As they passed the motel, Nelson pointed to a mauve station-wagon parked front-on to a unit.

'Wise-boy must've got in last night,' Nelson said. 'Time you get home from work — you bet he'll be waiting.'

'Once in Sydney's once enough.'

'You tell that to Wise-boy — what you gunna tell Iris?'

Mist hung over the sea and the Bay. Through mist the late-afternoon sun appeared as flat, as rayless, as red, as a school-Atlas illustration of Mars.

When the dented and rust-lichened utility truck reached the corner, Robby stepped from it. The truck rattled off the way it had come; and Robby walked past new two- and three-storey brick vacation flats, past up-on-stilts weatherboard houses of older Bay residents, toward a cluster of similarly constructed but paint-peeled houses beyond.

He passed the mauve stationwagon out front, and began to think of its owner not as Nelson called him — but as Warboy. As Mr Warboy at that.

Among stilts below a verandah, Mr Warboy was holding the punching bag while Nelson punched with such force that verandah floorboards above announced each punch with abrupt clatter.

Beyond was an area once the separate backyards of houses. From these the fences had been pulled down, making an enlarged communal area. Here Norman Prayta sat cross-legged, trying to pick out a tune on his guitar to the coaching of Celestina, her mother, and Rosie, while standing men passed a bottle.

'Must look after the working man,' Norman Prayta said. One of the standing men passed Robby the bottle. From Celestina's lap, Maxie toddled on podgy legs and Robby squatted to his son. The baby was not there. Nor Iris.

Celestina spoke to Norman Prayta, then ran on fat legs past where Nelson punched and Mr Warboy braced the bag, to the house beyond. This was the house Robby, Iris, Maxie and the baby had to themselves until those who had gone north for the sugar cane season returned. Celestina ran up the stairs to the verandah, and in at the flywire door. When she came out, the turned-up-loud sound of voice and guitar followed her like a wave. Norman Prayta bent over his guitar to take up the melody.

Robby hefted Maxie onto his hip, carried him up the stairs and in at the flywire door.

'Celestina took half of that strasbourg today,' Iris said. 'And Rosie helped herself to four tins of sardines.'

'They'll payback.'

'By looking after Maxie or the baby — not by replacing. Not with money! — *I* don't take from them!'

This was Iris's constant complaint. It set her apart

from the others of that cluster of houses, both those who lived there permanently and those who came and went. For them, possessions of any one of them were possessions of all.

Iris said: 'How we ever gunna get ahead?'

Robby had thought she'd got ahead — she had her console.

He followed her into the next room. On the floor was the baby. Iris went across to the combination record-player and wireless and television. She lifted the needle from the record.

'Hey!' Robby said. 'Norman's trying to learn that!'

Iris tossed the record among others on the floor. These were the Country and Western records bought by Celestina and Rosie and Norman Prayta, even by some of the men standing and passing a bottle.

'It's *my* console,' Iris said. She took a record from the storage space next to the television screen, placed that on the turntable.

Robby left Maxie on the floor beside the baby, went from that room and the kitchen, down the verandah stairs. He was followed by the voice of Julie Andrews turned up loud to assert ownership of the console.

Robby felt with his skin they were watching — Norman Prayta (his hands on the wood of his guitar), Celestina (her gaze a direct challenge), Rosie and Celestina's mother (heads bowed to couch-grass, but watching), the standing men (their pass-of-bottle become an action suspended) — none of them accepting or understanding Iris's assertion of ownership. Robby supposed it was the white part in her. But Celestina was part-white. And Rosie. He knew what they all said Iris needed.

Nelson stopped belting the bag. He brought Mr Warboy across. Each of the standing men shook Mr Warboy's hand, then Celestina.

'Mine's a Spanish name,' Celestina said.

'A Spanish man,' Celestina's mother said, nodding

her head of starkly white hair against asphalt skin. 'I don't remember his name.'

'I've had five kids,' Celestina held up fingers and counted them off. 'One from a Chinaman, one from one of our people, one from an Englishman with red hair, one from an Islander, one from an Italian man with a wife.'

'The Queen says us dark people should mix,' Celestina's mother said. 'Celestina mixes.'

Robby introduced Norman Prayta.

'My uncle,' Robby said.

'Ahh,' said Mr Warboy. 'Classificatory uncle?'

He's done reading, Robby thought. He must want me.

Nelson said Norman was their uncle like white-people's uncle: mother's brother.

Then Mr Warboy said he wanted Robby to put on the gloves with Nelson. Robby put on the gloves, and Nelson boxed fast, throwing a lot of leather, with Robby moving away and around him. Then Nelson threw a looping right-hander, and Robby stepped inside the looping arm, punched fast and hard into Nelson's body, then stepped out again.

'That's nice,' Mr Warboy said, putting an arm around Robby's shoulders. 'You're as good as I heard you were. Fast. And heady. Nelson's a bull — strong. But I wish he had your timing.'

Mr Warboy unlaced the gloves.

'With weight-training and isometrics we could build into you some of Nelson's strength, then sparring with all kinds of partners — I could take you places Robby-boy.'

Robby said: 'I been there.'

'That time Robby-boy, you had no trainer, no manager. But with me behind you — you'd make more in one year than you'd make in three on the railways.'

'The money'd be nice,' Robby said. 'But Sydney.'

He had gone to Sydney after three months with a

travelling boxing troupe. That was when Mr Warboy had three Australian champions and Nelson. He wasn't interested in an unknown even if he was Nelson's brother. Nelson was living at Mr Warboy's home, so Robby was on his own in the city. He got a few preliminary fights and won them. But never before had he been in a place without an horizon. And he did not fit in with any white people there nor with any black. Then he met a girl who was part-white and part-black. When she became pregnant, he married her, married her properly because that was what she wanted, and brought her north to the Bay.

'Sydney,' Iris said. She had the baby on her hip and she must have come down the verandah steps during the boxing. 'I'm from Sydney.'

'Aha,' said Mr Warboy. He started to turn back to Robby, when his head, his whole body, stopped in mid-turn. He stood looking at Iris alone on one side of Robby, then at Celestina and Celestina's mother and Norman Prayta and the rest on the other side. He moved to beside Iris.

'Nice place, Sydney.'

Iris said you could get ahead in Sydney. She'd a girl friend who had. She, the girlfriend, had a house she didn't have to share. It had a lawn and flowers and an elevated stove even and she, the girlfriend, was saving to put a deposit on carpet wall-to-wall.

'All costs money,' Mr Warboy said. 'But Sydney's the place to make it. What y' say Robby-boy?'

Robby said: 'You can't see the island.'

Mr Warboy laughed and Robby laughed. Iris clung to the baby. Maxie toddled to her, clung to her skirt.

Mr Warboy said: 'Sounds like your little lady would like to be back in Sydney.'

'Haven't the fare,' Robby said. 'Emptied m' bankbook t' buy the TV and record-player console she wanted.'

'No problem,' Mr Warboy said. 'I'm driving back

Sat'day night, home f' tea Sunday. You could all come with me.'

'Iris wouldn't leave the console.'

'Might fit it in.'

'Too big. An' I have t' give a full week's notice t' the railways or I lose holiday pay.'

'Tell y' what: Yer little lady 'n' kids come with me, you come by train next week. I'll pay y' fare. Should work out better that way — we'd all fit across the front seat, and with the back down we're bound t' fit in the console.'

Iris moved to beside Robby. She tugged Maxie in front of her so she could loop her arm through Robby's like whites did.

'What y'say, Robby-boy?'

Robby felt Iris against his arm. He could feel her heat. He watched an ant emerge from a runner of couch-grass to cross a patch of bare earth, and he pressed his foot on the ant.

'Wel-l-l, Robby-boy — no need for a decision right now. There's a couple o' days before Sat'dy.'

Robby lifted his foot and the ant began to run lopsided in crazy circles.

'You think it over, Robby-boy. You talk it over with yer little lady.'

Even on the smooth bitumen of the esplanade, the truck rattled. It rattled through late-afternoon flare of sunlight on bitumen, past flats, shops, the outdoor tables of a pub.

With his hands on the steering wheel, Mick said: 'When you gunna come to the island?'

Robby laughed. The question was at least half-joke. Others who worked at maintaining rail tracks regarded this white man and this black as two who worked together and who did those things for each other which made them a unit apart. Yet after work and at weekends their orbits did not cross, much less unite. Further, there was a discretion in their relationship which, for instance, caused Mick to stop his truck each night not outside the cluster of houses where Robby lived, but at the corner. And at the pub where blacks were served for Robby to acknowledge Mick though not to join him.

Mick had a boat. It was as barnacle-encrusted as his truck was rust-lichened, and the boat's timbers groaned as much as his truck rattled. But at weekends, if anyone brought a motor-bike and the rum and the stubbies, he'd take them to the island.

'Might be leaving,' Robby said. 'Might get m' picture 'n name in the papers like Nelson.'

'If you gunna leave, you ought t' come first t' the island.'

Robby's grandmother had been taken from the island when men on horses rounded up the Aborigines, then chained them to the deck of a boat that took them to a mission compound on the mainland, far north of the island. Later, a daughter and son of this grandmother moved south to where some few descendants of island and mainland tribes had come. Here they lived by morés that were not those of the whites among whom they lived, nor those of the dismembered tribes; though echoes of tribal life remained.

Sons of separate fathers, Robby and Nelson were born into the communal-living aborigines and part-aborigines at the Bay. Their mother left the Bay with an islander, and out of their lives. This left Norman Prayta with the awareness that a mother's brother should grow-up his sister's sons, yet unsure how this could now be accomplished.

Robby had never been to the island. In spite of his mother's mother, in spite of stories of the island which Norman Prayta had never known or had known and forgotten; in spite of weekend and mid-week boat trips for picnickers, he had never been.

He stepped from the truck, walked along past the mauve station-wagon, across the yard behind houses. Mr Warboy was bracing the bag while Nelson punched.

'I've measured the console,' Mr Warboy called. 'With the back seat down — it'll fit.'

Norman Prayta sat on couch grass, picking a tune on his guitar. He sang: *He-e-ea-vin is mai woman's luuv*. Beside him Rosie and some kids clapped thighs, while standing men passed a bottle.

Robby sat beside Norman Prayta and had taken the bottle — when at the house where he lived the flywire door exploded open to slam against the wall behind.

Celestina came out the door in a rush. She had tins and a packet in her arms. Iris could be heard shrieking after her. 'Buy yer own! Boong bitch!'

Then Celestina turned on the step to shout up: 'White blackfella!'

The door slammed shut. It exploded open again as Iris burst out onto the verandah. She had in her arms the whole scooped-up scatter of Country and Western records bought by Celestina and Rosie and Norman Prayta, by men absent for the cane season and men standing, now, without passing the bottle.

Iris swung an arm back, then forward. Across the open couch grass and sandy space a record sailed spinning. Again and again her arm swung back to send record after record spinning above the space.

Robby crossed the space, up stairs to the verandah where Iris swung an arm back then forward at each looping throw. Robby's own arm swung back, then forward and down. Iris crouched from him, one side of her face abruptly white beneath dark skin. Then she jumped to the verandah rail, lifted arms high, hurled down the records.

Robby watched the records plunge to the paving,

then explode outwards. When he turned, Iris had gone from the verandah. He stepped from the late-afternoon brightness, in at the flywire door to the sunless kitchen. In the instant of eyes adjusting to the dimness, Iris sprang. Her nail dug at his temples, raking down his cheeks. Someone (Maxie? the baby?) emitted a piercing wail. Robby grabbed for arms, gripped, forcing the arms down and behind her so that he had her against him and holding her arms behind. Against her writhing and kicking he held her like that as he propelled her across the dim kitchen until their rush was blocked by whoever was on the floor wailing. They fell. He grabbed again for arms and wrists to keep her nails from his face and they rolled about in the doorway. He got hold of her wrists, then he felt her mouth at his neck and she was using lips and tongue, not teeth. He, realizing, let go her wrists to push her dress up, her pants down. Her legs locked around his waist, and he stood with her around him, lurching into the further room. They tripped again when the other that began wailing stopped his legs. With Maxie and the baby both wailing, they tottered, they fell, laughing. Laughing and plunging together.

Later, he awoke. The dimness inside the house that opposed the glare without, now had become gloom that pervaded inside and out. Beside where he lay on the floor, Iris slept with her head on his chest. The baby had crawled to where her dress was torn, exposing a breast, and slept there. Among records in covers that had been pulled or had fallen from the console, the dark mound that was Maxie lay sleeping.

Beside Iris and the baby he lay stark awake. He saw the gloom turn to dark, then dark crossed by moonlight slanting from a high window to the opposite wall, creeping down the wall to the floor.

If Iris had brought him that tension which racked him between the people and place of which he was a part, and the gusty flare then cold then flare again of her loving, she had also brought the more constant warmths of her maternity. Now he remembered her sitting cross-legged on the beach, holding Maxie and finger-drawing in the sand for him. He remembered other nights, nights so luminous the light of the rising moon submerged the light of stars, the moon outlining the undulations of the island; and her slow smile opening on soft laughter that changed to shrill laughing as they chased along the beach, as they caught, mock-fought, tumbled in that entanglement of limbs from which the baby had begun.

With the suddenness of an alarm ringing, the question came to him: Had he started another baby?

With alarm deepening to dread he attempted to identify days and to count as Iris had told him. For as clear to him as moonlight was the knowledge Iris would not stay.

Within his hitting of her before the others was his ache that she submit to the morés of those others — within her talon-raking spring at him was her declaration that she would not, but would fight with such weapons as she had.

He lifted her head from his chest, stood, stepped over the sleeping Maxie, through moonlight to the door. He was aware of pain down one side of his face, but he moved quickly down steps and from the houses, along the path to where the shops began. He walked through cones of light from streetlamps above and between the outdoor tables of a pub and in at the glass doors.

Past men standing in groups, one man sat alone. His back was a curve continuous from bum on bar stool to elbows on bar. Beside him was one glass tall and one glass short, the liquid in both at half.

'Hey White Bastard — you gunna buy me a drink?'

The curve jolted to a straight line, the eyes staring for a moment at the speaker.

'Str-uth, Robby — yer bloody face!'
Robby asked: Did he have to buy his own?
Mick signalled the barman. No further word passed between them until after the barman pushed across the beer and helped himself from the scatter of change in front of Mick.
'Next thing we know,' Mick said. 'You'll be comun t' the island.'
'Buy me a rum too,' Robby said. 'An' I'll let y' know.'

On a bench outside the cabin, he lay listening to the *peew-peew-peew* of curlews on the island.
While others had been fishing on the tide's slack and the moon was behind cloud, he had seen a beach crossed by logs stacked for shipping by barge, and trees sloping up and away on hills beyond. When the tide began its run, the two who had come with Mick and himself cleaned bream, then took from the ice-box a stubby each and went into the cabin. Mick took out a bottle of rum and he stood with Robby in the stern, each swigging in turn until after the moon went down.
Lying on the bench, Robby felt rather than heard the tide reach its slack. Then the curlews ceased and whipbirds began, and it was morning.
On two motorbikes fitted to hold the tall rods upright, the four rode along tracks between mangroves then rainforest until that ended in bare dunes reaching to sand cliffs sparsely treed with pandanus. They rode the sand cliff ridge with beach and ocean below. Behind cabins they passed a dump where crows picked among bottles, tins, punctured cans, papers, discarded kerosene fridges, motor bike frames, scales and skeletons of fish, tangles of rope and line. Back of the beach were sheds and machinery with pumps disgorging a dark slurry into tanks sunk in sand. De-

scending to the beach, they rode between the surfs spumy run-in and roll-back, and where the tides apogee was lined in sea-wrack and mainland rubble.

Where head and shoulders of rock butted into the sea, rods were rigged with lures. The two stayed below on the shoulders of rock, while Mick climbed high on the head to scan through binoculars for school tailor.

Robby had climbed with Mick, then he continued on down to a further beach. This margined a shallow bay curving from one sea-butting head of rock to another.

Toward this further head of rock, he came to the middens. He stood looking to the beach where hill-ocks of shells rose up out of sand. Then his gaze turned to birds wading in the shallows. The birds and the middens would go together, he thought. Stand-ing where the birds had stood, he swivelled his hips to auger his feet into sand until he felt the shells of eugaries beneath his feet. He carried the eugaries to a midden, where he broke open the shells. He ate the fish inside, then threw the wet-glistening shells onto the sun-calcined shells of the midden.

High on the head of rock, the mouth of a cave gaped. He climbed to this shallow cave where he found ashes among the sand of the floor and soot on the roof. There were also hands. Red ochre outlined the shape of hands on the white rock — hands of children, adults, youths, that once had lived there. One hand had a finger missing, and some seemed to have extra fingers until he realized one hand had been stencilled over another. He held his own hands flat on the rock among the hands outlined in ochre; and he stayed in the cave through late-morning, noon, afternoon.

He dreamed of womens' laughter at their own hip-swivelling dance to auger feet into sand for eugaries — of men launching bark canoes to hunt dugong and turtle and mullet, of girls returning at nightfall with the fruit of pandanus and with honey vesselled in bark, of fires and of feasting and men dancing with feet apart and thighs quivering, boys at man-making stamping and stamping the red glow of coals, old people at mourning gashing their chests, gashing their shoulders, of the lore of beach and forest taught from mother's sister to sister's daughter, the love of tide and turtle and mullet and dugong taught from mother's brother to sister's son, and in telling from mother's sister to sister's daughter and mother's brother to sister's son by which the stories endured.

It was dark when the bikes were passed from the dingy into the boat and the dingy tied behind. The two prized caps from stubbies, talking loudly, laughing, as they lifted the lid from the ice-box to look at the fish inside.

Mick had his head and arms and the bottle of rum out the cabin hatch as he steered. Twice, he called, holding out the bottle.

Twice Robby shook his head. He stood watching the widening arms of wake reach back to the island. Dump of sea wrack and mainland rubble, ravaged by loggers and sandminers, its lore and its stories all but forgotten. Yet the island was there — still there. And while daily seen there by him, it redeemed to him the whole of his blood's story.

Sunlight flared on the bitumen wet from rain in the night. Nelson and Robby ran at the edge of the bitumen, the sounds of their running seeming to hang in the early-morning stillness. They ran from the road, beneath high eucalypts in the caravan park, to the beach, running on hard sand at the water's edge.

Nelson said: 'Brother, what y' gunna do?'

About what, Robby did not ask. He had returned from the island to find the house without light. Iris might be in one of the other houses and Maxie and the baby sleeping. But in the bed in the kitchen was neither Maxie nor the baby. Then he passed to the next room — and he saw that the console was gone.

For that night and the next he had stayed in rooms where the console was not, where Maxie, the baby, where Iris were not.

Throughout two nights he had lain stark awake, evoking the inner-emptiness of the city. Of where there was no rim of sky, of where even his dreaming could not glimpse the distant undulations of the island.

'Iris told Wise-boy you'd come. An' he left the fare.'

Out at sea a mist withdrew beneath the risen sun, revealing the deep deep blue of the island.

Robby said: 'I tell you this, brother — I never leave this place.'

Yet as he said it, he knew the emptiness he had evoked on two nights was but one emptiness.

When Nelson stopped running to shadow-box, Robby ran on. He ran, though the nights without sleep had taken his running from him and breath burned in his throat with a taste of nausea, he ran. Running from a voice that called after him, a voice that was Nelson's yet seemed to be his own, a voice pursuing him, calling. 'What y' gunna do, brother? What y' gunna do?'

Vera

Within the supermarket, gloom without coolness pervaded the shelves and the aisles between. Where the gloom deepened at the *Cold Meats* end, Vera was changing numbers on the price stamp. She looked up to see him coming toward her between *Pet Foods* and *Detergents*. Closer, she saw his nice tan on limbs, cream towelling shorts, hibiscus pattern on shirt, strong even teeth parted in a half-smile as he spoke.

'Where're the bread rolls?'

She moved ahead of him to the wire baskets. Then they stood, each not quite looking at the other.

'Name's Arthur,' he said. 'Travelin' the coast, sleepin' in m' car.'

'No reg'lar job then?'

'As reg'lar as five years of thirty-seven an' a half hours a week cookin' peanuts . . . Now I'm one week o' holidays down an' three t' go; an' I'd ask you t' show me the Bay only I reckon yer boyfriend might kick-up.'

'Mightn't have a boyfriend,' she said.

And then: 'Or might have. Only he's away.'

'Wel-l-l-l?' he said.

'Don't count on it.'

But after he stepped out into the brightness, she took hairspray and makeup and eyeliner for Roslyn to ring up on the register.

She had seen the car in which he had driven from the opposite curb; and through the languid afternoon she watched for its return.

When the hands of the clock passed five-thirty, Vera kept stamping prices. Not until Roslyn and Dorrie came out from the change room did Vera go in. It was past six when she came out. She walked between shelves stacked with tins, with packets, her step buoyed on the white-girl-pretty image that had looked back at her from a change room mirror.

Reaching the door, she felt a moment of heaviness. But the feeling of buoyant lightness returned as she pressed her back against the door until she heard the lock click shut. Lightly, lightly, she ran across bitumen in shadow to the waiting white slope-back Valiant.

They drove around the Bay, then to a drive-in theatre. When a sea mist came between the car windscreen and the bright blown-up images on the screen, they drove to a park overlooking mudflats and sea. Arthur's arm was around her shoulders and they kissed. She felt a hand in movement on her thigh. Her own hand took that hand away.

Looking out at mudflats and the distant row of lights through mist that was the jetty, Vera said she reckoned he'd be moving along the coast next day.

'What d'you think?' Arthur asked.

Vera said she wouldn't know.

Arthur started the car. Following her directions he drove away from the jetty end of the Bay, past lawns and gardens of poinsettias and pandanus. He stopped the car where she indicated: at a driveway beside which stood a concrete burro with sombrero at the street-front edge of lawn.

He leaned across her for the doorhandle, forearm touching the bareness of her upper arm.

'Hey,' he said. 'I'll stay.'

Within backstep shadow, Vera waited until the receding sounds of Arthur's car no longer reached her. Then she left the shadows of her aunt's home to begin four kilometers on foot to her own.

That day, Vera had carried into the supermarket the

biggest cardboard box she could find among the storeroom jumble of discarded boxes and cartons. She filled the box with groceries, with tins of sardines, loaves of bread, bottles of Coke, lengths of cabana and strasburg. When she paid Roslyn at the register, Roslyn said (as she did each payday) — she was a fool.

From the Liquor Department, Vera took bottles of Brandivino, took money from her pay envelope. Dorrie said (as she said each payday) — she'd never learn.

But Dorrie and Roslyn both helped her drag the overflowing box to the door for Norman Prayta when he came in whichever car or truck he managed to borrow.

Now Vera kicked off thongs. She ran from her aunt's home, her bare feet slapping on concrete footpath and bitumen road, then carried her over couch grass margining the esplanade, to the beach.

There her run stopped. She stood looking at ridges of waves, starkly white in the darkness.

She wondered if any of the groceries or the sausage or bread or Coke had been left for her. Among the Aborigines and part-Aborigines with whom she lived, borrow-and-payback was so much a part that ownership was barely recognized. Now she felt resentment rise like nausea within her: resentment toward her work supporting those who did not work, toward many who did not want to work, toward those who cashed welfare cheques wholly on rum and Brandivino.

This was not the first time such resentment had risen within her. One morning she had gone with Larry as he drove from the Bay. They drove all morning to reach where midday glare was thrown back from corrugated iron humpies beyond a town dump. That this visit to his maternal uncle was important to Larry was tangible in the whole bottle of Bundaberg

Rum he brought as a present; that the visit was presumed important to Vera was expressed in the quite formal handshake of the uncle.

Though the uncle's sense of occasion moved him to strive for such formality of manners and dignity of bearing as a man could achieve among low corrugated iron humpies with red dust floors and wheatbags for beds; it was the woman with whom Vera drank rum from peanut butter jars, whose image became incised on Vera's mind. Larry's aunt wore a discarded man's suitcoat over a too-long cotton dress to which kids clung or in which they buried their faces. Her cheeks were sunken, her mouth drawn in on sparse-toothed gums, scalp showing through graying straggles of hair — at little more than thirty, already old.

As Larry drove the borrowed truck back to the Bay, he sang. Not only had his maternal uncle accepted his wife-to-be — he had been fulsome in congratulation.

For Vera, the rum and the distance brought drowsiness. With drowsiness came a starkly vivid image of Larry's aunt. It was an image strangely abstracted from the person. Above the too-long cotton dress with its clinging and face-burying kids, above the man's cast-off coat, the face with its sunken cheeks and sparse-toothed gums seemed not the face of Larry's aunt — but Vera's own.

Larry had left by train to go north for the sugar cane cutting season. The abstracted image of her own face looking out from the face of Larry's aunt was with Vera as she began the four-kilometer plod of beach that would take her beyond the mist-shrouded lights of the jetty, to her home.

Each night of that week and the two that followed, Vera stepped from Arthur's car outside the mowed and clipped lawn, the drive-side burro with sombrero, of the home of her aunt. Each night she waited in back-step shadows, ran from there to walk the beach until the jetty lights were behind her. Beyond the jetty was the cluster of up-on-stilts houses of those Aborigines of the Bay who lived communally.

On their first Saturday together, Vera had Arthur wait for her at the supermarket at midday then drive to a beach far from where locals gathered. Outside her aunt's home that night, Vera said he should not come there for her next day. She would go early to a shop to buy for their picnic. He should meet her at the shop.

That Sunday they drove to where boats with outboard motors are hired. They swam, they wandered along beaches: all day, alone on an island.

Most lunch hours, he was waiting. When once he did not come, she walked past shops and was passing the outdoor tables of a pub when she saw him. She began to pass between tables — when she saw with whom he was sitting. She pivoted — hip colliding with table rim — to rush between tables, to run past shops. The pain in her hip was submerged in question. Had Norman Prayta and Harry Amungara seen her? Had they spoken of her to Arthur?

That night Arthur apologized for not meeting her during her lunch hour.

'Met fellas,' he said. 'At the pub.'

Guardedly she asked: 'What fellas?'

'Fellas I reckon you wouldn't know.'

Then he said an old guy had told him there'd be no moon and a full tide on Saturday night, and if they went in the afternoon and fished into the night they'd catch a stack of bream. She didn't mind if he went did she?

That afternoon Vera left the supermarket to follow the route Arthur took each night. She had never been to her aunt's home in daylight. She had never been inside. Her house (so told to Arthur and so her description went) housed her crippled and widowed mother who watched TV and listened to stereo records and a man came each week to mow the lawn with an electric lawnmower.

The electric lawnmower at least existed. When Vera reached the concrete burro with sombrero, her aunt was crossing the lawn and back behind the electric lawnmower. Her aunt stopped. Motor whirring, cord in hand, her aunt stared. The stare moved from Vera to glance along street and footpath, to check neighbouring lawns, driveways, front windows. Only then did she jerk her head, gesturing Vera behind the house.

Vera followed the concrete driveway to back steps and out of possible sight of neighbours and passers-by.

'What y'want comin' here?'

Vera's silence was taken for reproach: if the Rainbow Serpent and Parrot-fish Man had long since expired from those among whom Vera lived and from whom her aunt had delivered herself, the obligations of a maternal aunt had not.

When Vera did not answer, her aunt went in at the flywire door. Vera followed to stand within the unfamiliarity of chrome and formica, of white enamel on 'fridge and freezer, of a stove with dials and a window front.

From a ledge above the stove her aunt took what Vera knew to be a bankbook. The book was opened, thrust toward Vera.

'I work an' I work an' Ronald works an' works an' the money goes in there.'

The book was held so close Vera could not distinguish the numbers, only that there were a great many of them.

Her aunt's statement of her own and of her husband's industry was accepted by Vera; for though her aunt seemingly never saw her, Vera daily saw her aunt: her Islander-frizzy hair always coiffured and ribboned, her Aborigine-asphalt cheeks always powdered, the aunt served behind counter at the Bay's haberdasher by day and from a picture theatre ticket box by night. Her white husband gunned petrol and washed windscreens on weekends after his week of clerking at the Gas And Fuel.

'In there,' her aunt said, snapping the book shut. 'An' it comes out only for a new Torana with cassette-player 'n' leopard skin seat covers this year an' carpet throughout next . . . Now you come thinkin' 'cause yer m' sister's daughter an' marriageable I oughta give yer some. Well I'm tellun you, when I left the mob an' married Ronald, I finished with that stuff.'

The bankbook was slapped back on the shelf. Vera began to arrange in her mind words with which to tell her aunt that was not why she had come (and other words — words giving her reason for coming). But already her aunt was saying:

'What I'll give you is advice. I've seen you getting wise: goin' with that white boy. You're a good-looker an' so light if y' wasn't livun with the mob no one ud guess yer mother nor yer mother's mother neither. But you got no chance t' live proper while y're livun with them boongs.'

Her aunt smiled at using that word. A word considered, now, too inelegant even to be used by whites.

'So if y' wanna live proper — leave 'em. Leave them no-hoper boongs an' marry that white boy.'

Now there was no need to arrange words giving reasons. Vera had what she came for.

Having that, Vera returned to the up-on-stilts houses beyond the jetty. That night she sat on the highest step to the verandah, looking down on women and kids sitting on the sandy couch-grassed ground, singing Country and Western songs learned from transistor wirelesses. There was a second group, mostly men, the players and barrackers of two-up: players who, when one lost his money another would pass money to him to keep the game going; money not seen again, unless present winner became future loser and money was passed to him.

To Vera, distanced as she was from what she had been a part most Saturday nights of her life, the game seemed without purpose. If played as whites played — where winners kept their winnings and could buy, say, a 'fridge or T.V., perhaps a stove with dials and a window front — only then would there be some purpose or reason for the game.

Vera looked among the players and barrackers of two-up for Harry Amungara. The old man was not there. He rarely was on a night of moonless high tide. His absence would be followed by a day when all ate from his catch of bream.

The morning would also bring women lying in bed calling to each other from room to room, even from house to house. Their calls recounting the previous night — and the day's gossiping had begun. But Sunday's, sharp at nine-thirty, all gossiping would cease. Then hands groped beneath beds for transistors. From room to room, house to house, every wireless would be turned on — and turned on loud — to the Country and Western Hour.

The previous Sunday Vera had been beside Arthur in his car when from the wireless came the familiar sounds. Arthur sang along, *Heaven i-is mai woman's lu-uv*. Singing, slapping the steering wheel to the beat. He asked Vera if she liked Country 'n' Western.

'No! No I don't!'

Within the question, Vera apprehended a threat.

'No, I like . . .'

Unable to think what it was she should like, she pushed and pushed at the push buttons of the car wireless.

'Oklahoma!'

She had suddenly recalled records on supermarket shelves.

'Oklahoma and — Sound Of Music!'

On the Sunday that followed, Vera was stooping for a shell among the high tide line of broken shells and coral, when the realization descended on her that at this time next Sunday Arthur would already have left the Bay.

The week passed with Arthur waiting for her each lunch hour. Each night they drove to the drive-in theatre, or to watch a cane field being fired, or they walked along beaches deserted but for fishermen. They talked of fishing, of people who came to the supermarket, of the peanut growing country some three hundred kilometers inland from the Bay.

Had Arthur been one among whom she lived, Vera knew what she would do. But the change-room proclamations of Roslyn and Dorrie held her.

'A girl should never let a fella,' Roslyn had said, 'till he puts a sparkly on her finger.'

And Dorrie: 'Once she's got that — it doesn't matter. Then she's got him.'

One lunch hour they stood in front of a jeweller's window. Arthur, pointing, asked if she liked sapphires.

'Yes,' Vera said. 'Oh yes. Girls who reckon on a diamond ring are just . . .'

(She stopped herself from saying 'Gettin' flash').

'. . . just waistin' money.'

Arthur spoke of returning some weekends and at Christmas.

Future weekends may well be later than Larry's return from the northern cane season. Christmas would certainly be later.

To this anxiety, was added another: the knowledge

she could not keep deceiving him. She was certain he liked her enough and wanted her enough to accept the full dark blood of her mother's mother and her mother's mixed blood as well as the white part. If she could find the courage to tell him, and he accepted the mixture of bloods with her — then she would put aside the change-room proclamations of Roslyn and Dorrie, sure of her power to hold him with ways that she knew.

On the last day of Arthur's stay, they drove from the supermarket at midday. They watched a cane field being fired, then drove to a beach to watch the tide retreat across mudflats and birds glide in for the pickings. At nightfall, Arthur left her. He returned with prawns and a wine that fizzed, though the wine gave no effervescence to their mood. A breeze began to blow cold from the sea and they crossed sand and couch-grass to where the car stood. One side of the car was in soft darkness beneath trees, the other in yellow light from an esplanade street lamp.

Arthur slid past the steering wheel. Abruptly he said there was something he had to tell.

'No,' she said quickly, cupping a hand over his mouth. 'Something *I* have to tell.'

Then in a rush she told him.

He took her hand from his mouth, and he was laughing.

Laughter — not of derision, but relief. He put an arm around her shoulders, pulling her to him.

'That's funny,' he said. '*Real* funny!'

One arm holding her to him, his other reached into the glove-box.

'Real, real funny.'

Laughing, he took from the glove-box a packet and began tearing off the wrapping.

'I was near sick with worryin'.'

He took something from the box, fumbled to take hold of her fingers.

'Worryin' if you'd mind 'cause I'm quarter-caste. And you — you're -'

'What?'

'Quarter-caste. I was worryin' m'self near sick. And you — you're half!'

'Quarter?'

Then after a time filled with his soft laughter, she said: 'Islander?'

'Islander!' Arthur laughed and laughed.

'Abo?'

'What else?'

Laughing. Still laughing. 'What else?'

The abrupt pivot of her shoulders toward the door knocked whatever it was his hands held from them. She was wrenching at the door handle, kicking open the door. When her feet were on couch-grass, she swung around to him.

'You think I'd let *you*?'

Within her face lit by yellow light the lips were drawn back as though in pain.

He reached for her. But as his hands touched her arms, she did something the violence of which unnerved him. She drove her teeth into her lower lip with such force that instantly there was blood spilling down her jaw and against her teeth's whiteness.

'Boong!' She screamed. 'No-hoper boong!'

Arthur remained with arms outstretched as she backed from him. Then he slumped behind the steering wheel. From there he watched her, framed in the rear-vision mirror.

At the edge of road she stood within the cone of yellow light from the streetlamp above. For a long time she stood there; then she went on. She walked a few steps, stopped, walked, stopped, in the roadside gravel.

Till morning Arthur sat behind the steering wheel.

At half-light he began searching beneath the seat. He left the car to walk across beach and mudflats.

Already there were people with buckets and pumps, stooping to pump yabbies for bait. Arthur walked past the bait-gatherers to the sea's edge. What he had found under the car seat, he threw into the sea.

He drove along the esplanade, past the jetty and the up-on-stilts houses. Then he saw that Harry Amungara with whom he had caught bream on a moonless night. The old aborigine was carrying a red plastic bucket and a hoe with rake prongs to dig for sandworms. He was walking toward the tidal mangroves.

Arthur stopped the car. He tooted and waved. At the sound of tooting, Harry Amungara turned, peered to recognize, then waved in return.

Hunched over the steering wheel, Arthur drove. He turned from the esplanade, taking the road inland. For an hour he drove like that, hunched forward. But at nine-thirty he reached for the wireless. He switched on, pushed buttons until he had the *Country and Western Hour*.

Then he settled back for the long drive inland.

Tommy Garrett's Name

On Tommy Garrett's reckoning, living all but the first few of his sixty-two years on Bass Strait islands must surely have rendered him as immune to surprise as the smell of mutton bird is to soap and water. Yet in the lounge of this Launceston pub, he stood numbed by surprise.

He'd come in with the tide to bump his case along deserted Saturday-morning footpaths, reckoning on a good four-hour snooze after part of a day and all of a night aboard an island cattle boat. He hadn't bothered to undress, just kicked off his boots and lay on the bed.

Next thing he knew, Jake the barman was banging on his door.

'Lady t' see y'.'

He pulled on boots and descended stairs. The solitary occupant of the lounge sat at a laminex-topped table, a coffee cup in front of her.

She greeted him by name, gave him her own (which instantly he lost), pronounced herself his sister.

His years had been as sisterless, brotherless, as motherless, fatherless, as a ship's cat.

'Not a full sister,' she was saying. 'Half. Different dads, same mum.'

He stood, numbed to unresponsive inertia.

'I can see I've given you a jolt,' she said. 'Please — sit down.'

He sat. He saw that his self-pronounced sister (what *had* she said was her name?) was perhaps a half-dozen years younger than he, shortish, tending to squareness at the shoulders like a man, but with a bosom that was unmistakably feminine. Already the self-possession with which she was conducting this interview, daunted him.

'I'm not very subtle,' she said. 'So I might as well clobber you with the lot.' (Her name? Her name?) 'Mum's still alive. Though she might not be much longer. She said to me, Elsbeth. (Ahh!) before I go I want to see him again.'

Possessing not a glimmer of maternal memory, he could only react by turning her last word into a question.

'Again?'

'Oh, she's seen you before. In fact, quite often.'

Buffeted by gust after gust of surprise, he grasped only that behind one mystery there stood another.

'How did you know I'd be here?'

'But we always know. When island people come to town by boat they always stay at this pub.'

These days all but a few came by plane and stayed at motels. Still, those few who still came by boat did stay here. It was also true that when people from Flinders Island and from Cape Barren Island — and in earlier times from Clarke and from Preservation and from Chappell Islands — said they were going to town, they meant always and only one place — Launceston.

It seemed to him she had not fully explained; but before he could form any further question, he heard her say:

'I could take you now.'

'Where?'

'To Mum.'

His response was — not to respond.

'My Mum,' she said quietly, 'And yours.'

Staring at the laminex top of the table, he extended the silence.

'I've clobbered you with so much,' she said. 'It's no wonder you're stunned! . . . Now I'll tell you something else. While waiting for you I got so nervous I spilled this coffee. I was shaking so much! My poor hanky — look!'

She displayed the brown-sodden specimen — and suddenly her daunting self-possession was gone and she was laughing.

So was he. Their joined laughter went on and on until she had to wipe her eyes with the bedraggled handkerchief.

When their linked laughter was spent, a residue of warmth remained. A sister, he thought. A mother too.

And he wondered if before this day was done, would he find himself with aunts, uncles, nephews, cousins, brothers, a father — at sixty-two to find himself with the whole pattern and tangle of family.

He realized he was still sitting, she standing.

'Well,' she said. 'Coming?'

She swung the car out of the pub driveway, driving confidently and with concentration. Her concentration was a barrier to conversation, and he looked out at cottages in regimental lines up and down the steep curve of hills, at the three rivers which came to town to meet among gorge and preserved bush and ordered parkland, at commercial and government buildings of patriarchal solidness.

He supposed he had been born in this city. Or near it. His first memory was of the red brick and spear-tipped fence of the city orphanage.

He remembered a day when he was nine years old and he and others were kicking newspapers rolled and tied to make a 'football'. A strongly-built, square-jawed woman stood all morning inside the iron fence, watching them. When the bell rang for them to go inside for bread and dripping and tea, she called him to her.

He went with her to the office. Next day he went with her on board a boat loaded with empty barrels and unfilled woolbales. The boat sailed out from the city, along the river. They put in at Georgetown and it was night when they put out through the Tamar Heads.

During his life he was to travel that way many times, but he never lost what that first journey gave him — a sense of wonder.

For a time the boat followed lights on the shore until the darkness ahead was pierced by a revolving light in the sky. Other passengers went below — he continued to stand in the stern, for now they were going away from the revolving flashes of light. Just when it seemed they would pass into absolute blackness, a new light appeared ahead. Then he stood in front of the wheelhouse, watching the steady beacon grow toward the boat as it plunged on through blackness.

He was still standing there when daylight came to the sky. That was when he first saw the islands.

Great mountain peaks and ranges reached up out of the sea, some peaks joining sea and sky as they reached high into cloud. The sun flared on craggy tops even before it winched itself over the rim of sea. As the sun rose up, its brilliance crept down over precipitous rock, then across slopes where low foliage clung close against the ground. There were gentler slopes with tea-tree and tussocks back from indented coves and beaches.

Whichever way he looked, there were islands. Islands and islands beyond islands. The boat nosed unerringly between smaller islands toward a huge shoulder of rock that appeared quite naked of foliage. Closer, he could discern bone-coloured foliage clinging close to the slopes against the wind. The boat passed a headland and from here a quite different vista appeared. On this side the slopes were clothed in sheoaks, native pines, willows and tea-tree. Sheep cropped among tussocks on the lower slopes. There was a jetty, buildings, a fenced square of cultivated land.

'We're here.'

It was the square-jawed women who had come on deck and was standing behind him.

'This's home.'

Elsbeth swung the car between gate-posts of institutional red brick. They walked across the bitumen car park, and in at self-opening doors. Evidently his sister was known here, for she exchanged waves with the woman behind a counter marked ENQUIRIES and went on past lifts and up stairs, along a corridor with single bed wards going off on either side.

He, following, almost bumped into her when she stopped. She turned in at a door.

'I've brought him.'

Hearing her say that, he found himself being presented as though with fanfare and tarantara.

Confronting him was a grey-haired woman propped on pillows.

'Thomas.'

She reached out a hand toward him. Moving to her, he introduced himself as he would to any stranger.

'Tommy. Tommy Garrett.'

Looking at the hand he held, he stood amazed at its whiteness against his own.

'Thomas.' Her tone was an unmistakable reproof of "Tommy".

'And never "Garrett". Not while I had a say in it.'

'At the orphanage it was Thomas,' he said. 'Thomas Smith. More than half at the orphanage were called Smith.'

His mother gave a dry and wry guffaw.

He knew about "Garrett" and had wondered about "Smith". But if neither of these — then what? What *should* have been his name?

Garrett was the name of the woman who had taken him to the islands. She herself had been taken there as a bride; and she and her husband had built their home from island timber. They'd built their own furniture, too; their shearing sheds, sheep pens. Even the fenced vegetable gardens had to be solidly built because of wallabies, pademelons and what island people called badgers (wombats).

After their second wool clip was shipped out, they shipped in rolls of wire, kegs of nails, boxes of tea, bags of sugar, boxed tins of Golden Syrup, boots, trousers, dresses — commencing stock for the store they planned to build.

Island people began buying from them even before the store building was built. It was still uncompleted when Mrs Garrett's husband was returning from Flinders Island and became caught in what island people call a 'blow'. He was driven north toward the Vansittart Shoals. Not even wreckage was ever found.

It was Mrs Garrett who transposed 'Thomas' to 'Tommy', and instructed him in plowing, planting and digging potatoes and onions, in mustering and shearing sheep. He was the second boy she had brought to the island. The other was Norman, a deaf mute. It was Norman who initiated him in trapping and skinning wallabies, killing snakes, in shooting, plucking and gutting native geese, who first shamed him into thrusting his arm up to the shoulder into mutton bird burrows to grasp the fledgling there.

Mrs Garrett was a hard taskmistress to the boys and withheld herself from any display of affection toward them. Yet she was not without kindness. No work was performed on Sundays, and at dinner there was always something special — a whole Cape Barren Goose, or a king flathead or a saddle of wallaby, and afterwards dumplings with Golden Syrup.

He'd been four years with Mrs Garrett, when Norman came running to the house with wordless cries and outflung arm gesticulating toward the north of the island. Mrs Garrett and he followed Norman until they saw the three masts and iron hull of a ship stuck fast on the shoals.

There'd been a gale the previous night, though not of such intensity that island people would have called it a big blow.

Nor was that the only oddness. During his time on the island, Tommy had seen the look of men who had escaped the death's teeth of a gale. The men landing in lifeboats did not have that look. Not only had they escaped with their lives, but with food. And rum.

That night the rum was passed around as one sailor played on a squeeze-box, and others danced with Mrs Garrett and each other.

A week later the sailors were still there, though their mood of celebration was gone. A steamer had come up from Devonport and was trying to tow their sand-ballasted ship off the shoals. All that day and much of the next the attempt went on. When the steamer sailed away, the three-master was still there. One sailor who spoke English, clapped both boys on the back.

'Ve did goot — *ja*?'

His other hand descended onto Mrs Garrett's shoulder and pulled her toward him.

'*Ja* — ve did goot!'

When the other sailors left, this one stayed. He cut down trees, dragged the trunks down slopes to split with a maul and wedge. He set about finishing the store building. At night he played his squeeze-box and Mrs Garrett, that life-hardened woman, danced in the space between the table and stove. She also began showing affection toward the boys, particularly Norman. Laughing, she dragged him around in a clomping dance. The deaf Norman was unable to follow the music and would tangle his legs. Then the dance turned into a mock-wrestle with Norman and her rolling on the kitchen floor, while the sailor laughed and played his accordian.

From a country at the other end of the world, news reached them of an enquiry into the loss of the ship. Later, the sailor told them there was money for them in a Launceston bank. Mrs Garrett wrote out a long list and one morning the sailor took the list and Norman on board one of the island tramps.

When they returned on board that same tramp, part of its hold was filled with goods for the now completed store. The boat had put out through the Heads and had passed the Swan Island lighthouse. Some time after that, a really big blow struck. The tramp went down somewhere between the lighthouse and Clarke Island.

When the skipper of another tramp brought news of this to them, Tommy cried and cried. Mrs Garrett showed no grief. She seemed not to react at all. One day more than a month later, she stayed in bed. When Tommy took her tea and potatoes, she did not eat or drink. Five days later, she was still in bed and still had not eaten. Tommy climbed to the top of the range and lit two fires. The boat that this distress signal brought, took Mrs Garrett off.

Tommy was alone on the island for more than a week before an island tramp came to the jetty. The skipper told him Mrs Garrett had died.

'If you like,' the skipper said, 'You can come with me.'

Later he was to sail on every tramp working the islands and between the islands and the northern Tasmanian coast. But that time he stayed. He was alone on the island until a party of Cape Barren Islanders called at the island on their way to the outer mutton bird islands. He went with them.

'Elsbeth said you'd seen me before.'

His mother swivelled her head from facing him, toward his sister.

'You spoilt it!' Her accusation was quite theatrical. 'You knew I wanted to tell — but you had to get in first!'

'Mum — all I did was to give your performance a fanfare intro . . . Just like a compere on T.V.'

Their mother seemed immediately to accept this, for her head revolved back to him.

'Well then,' she lifted herself higher on the pillows, whisked back stray hair, smiled at him quite coquettishly. Evidently what he was going to hear *was* going to be a performance, a well-rehearsed one at that. 'After you went from the orphanage, I pestered and pestered the staff there until I learnt where you'd gone. When I found it was to the islands, I was glad. Years later, a girlfriend Dulcie, poor Dulcie, she married a Catholic, poor Dulcie had a job cleaning, making beds, at that hotel where you island people stay. She told me the first time you stayed there. When Dulcie shocked everyone by what she did and left Launceston, I mean, she really *had* to, there was always someone there who let me know. They were always very good to me at that place.'

'So that's where you've seen me, at The —'

'There? Heavens no! I've never seen the inside of a hotel in my life! . . . We lived out from town, past Exford, and there's a place where a point of rock juts out into the river. There's a red beacon light right on the point and —'

No longer was he listening. He was seeing again the river where it swelled out wide and shallow where hills sloped back from both shores. Then the hills came down in steep curves, confining the river between them. On one bank were houses, European trees among the native eucalypts, boat sheds, a jetty, usually a family fishing boat or two. The opposite bank was all native scrub. Stringy bark and tea-tree and native pine grew in tangled profusion on the slope; and at the base a tongue of rock licked out into the river, a red beacon at its tip.

He saw again the woman standing beside that beacon, waving as they passed. It was always on the outward voyage, and he had seen her there even when drifts of rain veiled the high tangle of scrub on the hill behind.

The island and north-coast tramps were manned by a skipper, a crew of two, three, occasionally four. At first there were jokes about the woman who waved, skipper and crew chiacking each other as to whose sweetheart she was. Later she was no longer a joke, but spoken of as someone revered though not quite flesh and blood — like a heroine in an often-told story.

Tommy Garrett came to town not only aboard the island tramps, but also in the flat-bottomed boats of Cape Barreners.

Descendents of Tasmanian native women and early sealers, they built their own boats. He'd gone with them into island forests to select and fell timber for the keel. He'd worked beside them at boat-building; and gone with them each year to the outer islands for the 'birding'.

Among white islanders and Launceston dockworkers, the seamanship of Cape Barreners was legendary. But big blows on Bass Strait and rip tides between islands took many of them.

Even when he was leaving Launceston aboard the small boats of Cape Barreners, the woman had waved from the point.

There'd been an interval of years when he had not come to town at all. He'd married and tried to farm stony acres between a swamp and the peaks of The Patriachs on Flinders island. Neither the farm nor the marriage had flourished. There were no children and his wife left for the mainland. He stayed. He returned to going with Cape Barreners to the outer islands for the mutton bird season; and going to town once or twice each year.

On these visits he liked to sit among the clatter of a busy cafeteria or among the noisy conviviality of pubs. He liked going to the pictures, to sit among the yell of kids at a Saturday afternoon matinee, or at night to see a celluloid tale of lovers in ball gown and evening dress to whom an elegantly-attired waiter brought an ice bucket and champagne and the couple raised glasses to celebrate their love — a world as far removed from his own as the Saturday afternoon exploits of Tarzan and Eskimo Nell.

It was more than a year after he recommenced these visits to town and he was leaving with the tide, that he again saw her, waving, where a point of rock jutted into the river.

He'd seen her since. Not every time and now not for some years. Yet she had become so much a part of his coming to town and going from it, that when she was not there, his imagination supplied her, beside the beacon, waving and waving.

'The fibs, the terrible fibs I told him,' his mother was saying. 'The reasons I invented to get out of the house and down to the point. The fibbing stories I concocted! . . . Yet in all else I was a good wife to him, Elsbeth's father.'

Then Tommy Garrett surprised himself. Preceded by no shaping of the question or inner-rehearsal, he heard himself ask, 'My father — who was he?'

His mother's spirited performance ended as abruptly as if a trap door had inadvertantly opened and the prima donna fallen through. Her head fell back on the pillow. Her eyes stared at him while time passed.

When she did speak, her voice was cold and rock-firm. '*Elsbeth's* father was a good man. Upright. Very straight.'

'Narrow,' Elsbeth said.

'Elsbeth and her father, they never got along.'

'What did you expect?' his sister said. 'Hanging a name like Elsbeth around my neck. It's straight out of an Illustrated Family Bible — a wilting virgin with a water pitcher on her shoulder! As soon as I could I rebelled against that name. I went into a training hospital because I'd heard nurses played up. The other student nurses there all studied diligently and worked hard. I worked hard too — but I *played* hard.'

'You were a monster!' their mother said.

'I wasn't going to wilt still wondering. And I wasn't going to hang a name like that on my own daughter. I named her Lola.'

The mother began a raucous titter. 'Lola.' His sister too began to splutter with laughter. 'And she payed out her once-sinful mother — by becoming a deaconess!'

The mother and daughter were both laughing. The mother's laughter had a note of gleeful vindictiveness. It seemed her life had provided no greater joke than this, the way Elsbeth's chick had found her roost.

After Elsbeth's laughter had subsided, their mother's went on and on. She was still laughing when he again put his question. 'What was his name — my father's?'

Her laughter dropped through the floor. She wilted against the pillow. Eyelids that a moment before had been wide, now drooped and closed.

Here, he thought, is her best performance yet. His sister came to his side of the bed, touched his arm. 'Come on.'

Aged mother or not, his impulse was to shake the old girl out of her sham.

He followed his sister. At the doorway, he glanced back and caught his mother quite openly watching him. She did not revert to her performance, but held his gaze with her own. 'The times,' she said. 'The time and the people — were hard.'

At the pub, Elsbeth's husband was waiting. The lounge was now crowded and a wireless was beefing out football. When Roy went to get drinks, Tommy Garrett asked what had happened to his father.

'Drowned,' Elsbeth said. 'Bass Strait. Though that wasn't the cause of bundling you off to that orphanage.'

Roy brought three beers and sat with them.

'I suppose,' Tommy said, 'They were never married.'

'They weren't.'

'I've often been told I was a real bastard.'

That ignited laughter in all of them and brought backslaps from Roy.

Supposing he'd been told as much as he ever would be, he was startled by a movement from Roy. It was intended as a private semaphore signal from husband to wife. But Tommy intercepted that signal. Its message read: STOP.

Elsbeth did not stop. She careered on against the signal. 'You must remember the times,' she said. 'It was a dreadful scandal if someone born Church of England or Presbyterian married a Catholic. Mixed marriages they called them then. As for what was later meant by "mixed marriages" — that was unthinkable!'

'People,' Roy said, having failed to stop his wife now careering along with her, 'People can be cruel.'

(Too right they could. He'd heard the Cape Barreners' home called Boong Island. And he'd heard the yarn told in pub after pub about a government agricultural expert sent to re-establish market gardens as an industry for the Cape Barreners. The yarn had it that six months after the experts left the island, two roos got through the fences and into the gardens. The roos weren't discovered for two weeks and by that time they died — of starvation!)

'Mum and your dad were set to get married,' Elsbeth was saying. 'Their intention was to go away after the wedding so people wouldn't count the months on their fingers. It was all planned, and the two families had a meeting to sort out wedding arrangements and expenses. The meeting was at the home of your father's parents', and they were very hospitable — crayfish and scallops and drink. Up until then there hadn't been the least suggestion of — of *anything*. But there was an uncle of your father's there, an uncle on the mother's side, and he wasn't just dark — he was black.'

'Black?' Tommy said. 'Black what?'

'Blackskinned. Really black. Almost blue.' Then Roy added: 'He must've been a genetic throwback. The family came from the islands.'

But he knew all the island families, the island names. Then what was his father's name? What should have been *his* name? He'd have asked right then — had not Roy created a diversion. Roy began energetically signalling toward the crowded bar, thrusting three fingers high, pointing down toward their empty glasses. 'Just when you need a drink,' Roy complained. 'You become invisible.'

Tommy said Jake wouldn't serve at tables when it was so crowded. He gathered up the glasses and went to the bar. When he asked for the bottles and for different glasses, Jake blinked. The barman kicked up a trapdoor behind the bar, scuttled down the steps.

All — he knew them all. All the names of that race descended from the twelve dark women that sealers had taken to the islands. During the century-and-a-half since, the families had all intermarried. Born into one, you were born into them all.

My people, he thought.

And then: Ohhh my people . . .

For he too had seen the neglected gardens, he'd heard the cruel laughter as people spoke of the islanders' home as Boong Island. Yet he'd been with his people when they pitted their boats and their lives against the eerie seas of the shoals on their way to the annual 'birding', as they set themselves against the sudden big blows, the mountainous seas, of Bass Strait — he'd been with his own when they had achieved some greatness as a people.

Taking the two bottles and the new glasses to the table, he no longer wanted to know into which family he had been born. That whole race ran in his veins.

When Elsbeth saw the bottles, she said: 'Goodness — bubbly!' Roy said: 'Celebrating, are we?'

Too right he was. He'd never before tasted the stuff, but he knew it was what townspeople drank when they were celebrating. And he knew what it was that they drank champagne to celebrate.

Love.

Mad Like Lasseter

Twice, now, he had come to the verandah, to stand gazing past the row of pines beside the drive to where the yellowish quartz-gravel track left the road and turned in at his front gate. He was waiting for Desmond to return, bringing Catherine. Catherine, he peevishly reflected, with her narrow hips and niggardly bosom.

At sixty-four a man should not be old, but he had come to feel old: when his lungs went on him and the coughing began. The tablets began, then, too, the injections, the eyes of his wife following him, the long drives north for the winters.

This morning, however, he was not aware of age. That presence had left him as he became buoyed on anticipation of the morning. Of this particular morning, for which he had schemed and stage-managed with a sense of occasion, almost ceremony.

A week previously he had told Desmond to bring Catherine on this day. He had avoided saying for what purpose; but Desmond would know. Oh, Desmond would know, all right. And when this day came, he had risen early, had taken cups of tea to the wife, then to Desmond. To wake him and remind him and to insist on the time. Ten o'clock Desmond had agreed. No later then, he had said, taking away the cup and saucer.

It was near eleven now, and he was still waiting. He was not sure about Desmond. He did not feel toward him what he felt a man should feel, what he wanted to feel, toward his son. 'A child of late loins', he had read that somewhere, and perhaps that was the trouble: the years between them too many and too different.

Part of what he had planned for this morning had already been accomplished. The lesser part. That part to do with the wife. Nance had her back to him and the reddened underneath of her arms flapped back and forth, just a little, as she rolled and rolled scone dough.

'Nance. Nance, y'know . . .' He coughed. 'Y'know I'm going t' show Desmond t'day . . . But y'self, Nance: there's what I've still got left. Not much of it that I'll needs-be touching. So, then, as well as the pension, when you need it — there it is. Don't sell it cheap, though. Not to a bank or a registered gold buyer: on the black where you'll get double the price.'

He held out to her a piece of paper. Her fingers smudged and scattered flour as she took the paper and held it at arms' length to read the name and the address there.

'Sell enough at a time t' make it worth his while, Nance; and you'll get double — more'un double! — what any bank 'll pay.'

She folded the paper and tucked it beneath the sleeve-band where it was tight against the plumpness of her arm.

'Don't you go overdoing it t'day,' she said. 'And don't expect too much of Desmond.'

Now he stood, waiting. He left the verandah to walk with deliberate slowness to the front gate and needlessly pushed it further back among the tussocks. He walked back along the drive, beneath dark arms of pine.

Roll of gravel beneath tyre-treads caused him to turn. A small grey sedan with hand-painted pink wheels, had turned from the road, between the gateposts; bringing his son and his son's fiancee to him, on this morning that was to span the years between.

It was a different car in which the three of them drove

over ironstone stained quartz-gravel, then bitumen, and again gravel. The three of them were silent across the front seat. It was seldom that he could find words to say to his son; which was odd, as he was a great yarner, a great teller of stories. Perhaps it was because of the months at a time without company that he became like that. He still carried in his pocket the gold he had smelted and melted into a sinker-mould and attached to a swivel and a wire trace. He had shown this in pubs and bush post-offices and, more recently, at northern caravan parks. He told people that he always fished with gold sinkers himself. The joke was not often a success for only the very knowledgeable and the very naive accepted it to be gold. However it enabled him to tell of Tennant Creek and the harsh Peterman Ranges and the still harsher Granites, of Chapman and Lasseter and what he had seen men do for gold.

Soon the track became narrow and began to rise and wind among flinty hills and scraggy gums whose foliage bucked and strained at their branches beneath clouds that flowed like a great grey river in air.

'Much further?' Desmond asked.

''Nother twenty, twenty-five, minutes. Then there's a stiff walk.'

Desmond was taller than he, though just as thin. But there are different kinds of thinness, and Desmond had not the sinewy wiriness of his own slight build. Desmond's nature was different, too. His five years of working life had been as a packer in a bacon factory, and since he started courting Catherine he had taken to religion. Catherine's father managed a supermarket he did not own and was a lay preacher.

He himself had never been one for religion, though he liked the stories well enough. He thought *Ruth* to be a story of great beauty and in life had known men with such a relationship, though never women; and in desolate places and with stores running out he had watched crows and had longed for the ravens of Elijah.

Now they followed wheel-tracks, then gaps between trees. He brought the car to a stop where the way was barred by scrub.

Desmond got out to stoop and peer along the front seat at Catherine staring fixedly ahead.

'You *could* wait in the car,' Desmond said.

'I *said* I'd come!'

Catherine abruptly slid along the seat and got out with the air of performing something that apparently *had* to be done.

Carrying the thermos and the bag of scones, he led them between spindly gums. The scrub ended at a hilltop and they passed an old poppet-head scarred black by fire, then they were enclosed within the wind-movement and sounds of scrub again. Twice, he stood waiting for Desmond and Catherine. He watched them climb to where he waited, climbing side by side yet linked neither by hands nor words.

The second time they climbed to where he leaned against a bank, he poured from the thermos and held out to them floury and crusty scones. There were mounds of quartz protruding from the leaves and long-abandoned shafts sunk to depths of ten and twelve and fifteen feet.

They reached where some fault or caprice among rocks had caused the side of the hill to be incised by sudden scarps of shale that dropped sheer for thirty or more feet. The incision was perhaps a hundred and twenty yards long. A few ferns grew precariously in cracks and in the narrow bottom.

Desmond and Catherine stood back from the edge of the scarp. He motioned them closer. Desmond edged forward a few steps; but Catherine was gripping his hand, now, holding him back.

'Desmond, my boy, you can come right to the edge: it won't cave. And you'll needs-be seein' the bottom.'

He stepped aside so they could stand where he had stood. The couple shuffled forward just sufficient to see over the edge by leaning forward.

'Wel-l-l, Desmond — there it is!'

His gesture was grandiose.

'There's your independence there Desmond. There's the end of you packin' in that bacon factory.'

The couple looked at each other and at the long incision in the ground and at him, as though the fault was not merely geological.

He had seen that look but walked quickly along the edge of the scarp. He eased himself over, his boots groping for footholds. Edging forward and down, he made a sudden leap and carried on by that momentum he stepped across a smooth face of rock then scrambled and slithered down a less severe face to the floor of the fault.

He stood among ferns, looking up.

The couple were stark against moving scrub and cloud. Catherine had slipped her arm through Desmond's and they were standing very close.

'You do it all in a rush,' he called up to them. 'There's no great risk.'

'We'll just watch,' Desmond shouted down to him. And then, still louder: 'We'll-watch-from-here!'

Not that shouting was necessary, as there was no wind between the walls of shale.

So there was nothing he could do except to point out to them where the reef was exposed and to uncover the trench he had dug along one side of the bottom and had covered with brush. He called to them that it was the same reef the shafts on the ridge were sunk onto; and that you could follow it for forty yards to where it 'blew' further down the slope.

To all this Desmond nodded tolerantly.

'It's only a narrow reef — nine inches in parts, never more 'un twenty — but the gold's thick enough t' dolly be-hand. That's what makes it worth workin':

you won't have t' put the quartz through a gov'ment battery — you dolly it y'self then get a good price on the black.'

'What's he mean?' he heard Catherine ask. 'What's he mean: *on the black*?'

But Desmond was calling down to him: 'Dad, this's real int'resting f' Cath t' see — isn't it Dear? — She's never seen anythin' like this. So it's real int'restin' f' her.'

'Desmond! — This's no Tennant Creek, this's not The Granites — the gold peters-out b'fore the reef blows on the slope. But there's enough here, Boy. Enough t' set y'self up.'

'Set-m'self-up?' Desmond's voice rose to a high pitch of incredulity.

'I'll give y' the paddock next t' the house, then six months, nine months, work here — and *there's* yer independence.'

'But how?' Desmond's note rose higher, higher. 'How?'

'Six months, nine months work here an' you could start a poultry farm.'

'What?' he heard Catherine. 'What's he saying?'

'He said a poultry farm.'

'*Poultry*!'

'Desmond! — It's yer independence that's here! It'll be the end of havin' t' say yes-sir, no-sir, in that bacon fact'ry. An' as soon as the poultry's bringing in a good return — you can build yer own place. 'Stead of havin' t' live with her parents and havin' t' say grace over tinned salmon!'

Catherine stepped quickly back; but Desmond stayed silhouetted at the edge to call down at him.

'Look, Dad, I've told and told you: it's all right at the factory. What's more, there's a chance — a *good* chance — I'll be able t' work with Cath's dad. Then at the supermarket I'll be a department manager.'

'Manager?' he shouted up. 'Managing — what?'

'Small Goods.'

'*Small* Goods!' His voice was pitched as high as Desmond's had been. But it was not incredulity that carried it to that pitch: it was derision.

'Desmond! — It's yer future that's here — don't y' see?'

'I've *got* a secure job an' there's the chance of a better one. At the supermarket there's a long-service leave, superannuation -'

'Desmond, if it wasn't f' men scratchin' in the bush there'd be no bacon fact'ry and no supermarket and no tinned salmon!'

'Orright, Dad! Orright! But that kind o' livin' is all past. No one lives any more the way you did. Men've walked on the moon — yet here you are like a brontosaurus that popped up in a cow paddock!'

'It was men scratchin' rocks in the bush that made this country!'

'If you ever cared f' the country you'd never have done what you've always done — sold on the black. All the gold you ever got — all *out* of the country!'

'Desmond, m' boy . . .'

But he suddenly turned. Grasping and slipping and scattering shale, he climbed with hands and feet and knees up the slope. He had felt the sudden rise of anger, for it seemed to him that men on the moon were a part of his side of the argument — not Desmond's.

At the top, he stood: confronting the couple. Now he was aware of his own breathing. It came rasping back and forth from lungs to throat, burning in his mouth with a taste of nausea. He stood. Breathing.

If Desmond had been stung to anger before, he was conciliatory now. Desmond's hand touched his shoulder.

'Dad, you're a hero, all right — isn't he, Cath? They make books and TV shows 'bout people like you. Like they did about the one you knew that died crazy in the desert.'

Lasseter . . .

Possom Lasseter!

Oh, Lasseter's death among blacks was the stuff of stories, all right; and little more than a year later he himself had followed into the Peterman's where Lasseter left his bones. Then north to Tennant Creek, north-west to The Granites. He had been one of the first there, at The Granites — Australia's last gold rush. And he had won much gold there, at the last and most desolate of gold fields, keeping some of it for years, to sell where and when he could get his price. He himself believed it was The Granites that Possum Lasseter had found and had died trying to find again. And perhaps he was lucky at that: to have died with the dream growing and growing even as he wrote he would trade a reef worth millions for a loaf of bread, and his bones fell apart.

Better that — than to have what you staked you life on rejected for a life of bacon-packing and small goods.

Along the track back to the car, he began to cough. The wind had eased and clouds no longer flowed like a river in air but piled on top of each other like great dark hills of mullock. He did not look behind. He knew *they* would be linked by hands, for their mingled voices reached him. And laughter, kept low.

In the car he had a spasm of coughing. When that passed he drove beneath a lowering sky.

Once he had read where a journalist or a politician had said that those who had died in the desert had not died in vain, for others with their spirit would follow and the country would be opened up and one day bloom. But that he no longer believed. He coughed and coughed for all who had lived among rock and deserts, who lived and died crazy with thirst and dreams; and whose manner of living and dying would go unredeemed in a world of Desmonds.

That night he would not eat. He sipped tea and the wife's voice came to him as though from a distance. He had overdone it again, she said. He always did, up there. And he had better have more than *one* good think about making that the last time.

In the morning, he lay in bed. He had always been an early riser; but the sight of Desmond taking his brown paper bag and his thermos of Milo to the bacon factory, was something he could not bear.

When he at last dressed, he walked out of the house and stood among wet grass behind the woodheap. Thin winter sunlight kindled a little warmth. The sky had been wrung blue by rain in the night. And from the night he had taken this honesty: that the manner of his living had been neither for a stripling son nor a stripling country. It had been for the living itself.

And he'd had that living. He had lived big.

Why, then, did he look for more?

But in his pocket his hand closed around the gold sinker with its swivel and the wire trace attached.

Ohh, the stories: the stories he had listened to and the stories he had *seen*; the hundreds of stories he had told: his own story told hundreds of times . . .

Nance called to him that his tea and his toast were getting cold. Then — they were stone cold now.

But he continued standing there, among sunlight on wet grass and on thistles. He was thinking of northern beaches, of men and boys fishing at the water's edge and from jetties, of couples lying close together on towels in the bright sunheat, of women and children running out of the sea to throw themselves down on warm sand.

North, he thought. Nance and he would go north. North, again, for this Winter.

The Bridge Pool

Neither of my parents were born country-people: some scheme of my father's caused us to move from an orchard-bordered road in what was becoming one of Melbourne's outer suburbs, to a landscape of paddocks that were sodden during one part of the year, and took on the colour of old bones at another. My parents bought five acres of land and a house on a back road, just past where it bridged a creek. Even then it was an old house. The walls were of hessian covered with wall-paper, so that switching on the light in the kitchen cast a ghostly half-light in the adjoining bedroom and passage. Buckets had to be placed to catch drips when it rained. It was only to serve until we could afford something better, and my parents set about brightening the window-sills and cupboards with paint and patching the roof with new iron.

The years we spent there must have been ones during which my parents were each, in different ways, coming to accept that this temporary accommodation might well become their permanent home.

For in time the yard behind the house became a cemetery for my father's failures: the death of his many schemes marked in headstones of rusting iron, two broken-down trucks, three long rows of empty chicken pens.

I remember my father, at that time, as being above average height, dark and thin, but with enormously strong hands. Within a community where deliberation was considered abnormal, he was much given to reflecting on the rightness of his actions, a preoccupation my mum blamed for his failures and which caused her to accuse him of moodiness.

What caused us to sell the urban house and go there, what scheme-fallen-flat that rusting iron was a memorial to, I have forgotten, or perhaps never knew.

The first scheme of my father's I can recall was chicken-raising. At the one-room school I was in the fourth or fifth grade, and for more than a year my father had been working at the council road-metal crusher. Then suddenly there were men with hammers in their belts and leather nail bags in front, lifting and hammering and calling to each other in our yard. Long wooden skeletons of sheds rose up where the potato paddock had been. The men left, and my father no longer went to the crusher each day, but worked with tin-snips and hammer against iron, hammer and saw against fibro plaster, covering the frames the men had erected. By autumn the pens housed chickens. Only a few at first, then hundreds, picking and squabbling, stretching their necks and trying their wings.

Things must have gone well, at first, for each Saturday of the spring of that year and the summer and autumn of the next, a truck loaded with crates of chickens entered at our drive. Crates of our chickens were loaded with others, then the whole swaying load would proceed out our front gate.

One Saturday the truck did not come. Instead, a white van turned in at our front gate. A man I'd not seen before asked for my father. He was slight, wore a suit and overcoat and had a smell like my mother's powder. He spoke softly and rapidly, telling my father the previous buyer had been bought out by Universal Specialty Corporation and he hoped my father would continue producing for them. He spoke of prices, and my father said he couldn't raise chickens for that. Then the man said my father's present set-up was inefficient. He needed cages to raise the chickens in. Cut fattening time by half. Universal

Specialty chickens never had their feet on the ground in their lives, never scratched in their lives, never moved more than nine inches at a time in their lives. 'That's the way t' do it!' Then my father said, 'Chickens — in fact anything — shouldn't be treated like that.' The man laughed. Universal Specialty were investigating the feasibility of producing white veal in this country, the man said. The vealers were kept tied to posts in dark sheds and fed only skim milk. Never see daylight, never taste grass, never move from that post in their lives. Produced a really white veal. Europeans were mad for it. It had big potential as an export earner. This country badly needed export earners and Universal Specialty would be doing its bit.

As he left, the man said my father was making a big mistake.

By the time the paddocks were slushy with winter rains, the only fowls in the pens were a few egg-layers, and my father was again working at the council crusher.

It was my mother who was embittered by this failure. She said it was just like the other time. And where had his moodiness ever got them except to put an end to any hope they might have had of getting out of the old house?

Getting out of that house was my mother's constant aspiration. And directly opposite was a house that mirrored, in terracotta and white, my mother's hopes. It belonged to our only near neighbours, the Platards, and was of clinker brick with a steep tiled roof housing an attic. A cypress hedge grew in front and a row of poplars lined each side of the long drive. And just as the house was a model for my mother's aspirations, so Mr Platard was a model of the community's: in that district of small-acreage farmers, he was accounted a successful man. Starting from a small holding, he had added to it until it was the largest in the district, then had put on a manager to run it for him. Since then, he had become stout, bought a new car each year, and had become so much the expression of popular opinion that he was never opposed at council elections. Having little to do on his own property, he spent hours in our kitchen sipping cups of tea and talking to my mother.

It was in comparing my father to Mr Platard that I began to see my father as a ridiculous figure. Mr Platard's success was as tangible as sheep and Chevrolet. While my father had only those rusting memorials to his schemes to show for his years.

Certainly my father was no part of any template I aspired to fit. For who would want to emulate a man whose efforts had all fallen flat?

So when my father returned from an auction one Saturday, and announced he had a new idea on an open-cut clay pit someone else had worked years before, and had bought a small crusher and an old Ford motor, I said I wondered how long it would be before they joined the other junk rusting in the yard.

We were all in the kitchen when I said that. I saw Mr Platard smile. My mother said, though without conviction, I *might* be growing up, but should at least show *some* respect. My father said nothing. He went outside. And we watched him, through the window, making peparations with planks and ropes to unload the means of his latest scheme.

Mr Platard nodded toward me, and addressed my mother. 'The boy's learnt a thing or two.'

'Let's hope he *has* learnt,' she said.

She looked out at where my father was wrestling with a strange piece of machinery on the back of the truck.

'Hopeless,' she said, shaking her head. 'Just hopeless.'

She began to laugh, her laughter thinned out to a frayed, mocking edge. Mr Platard's laughter joined hers.

I looked out: at my father struggling there against a background of empty pens and rusting iron, and my laughter mocked with theirs.

That was in early spring, and it was spring that the fisherman came.

One Saturday there was a utility truck parked between the bridge and our front gate. I had been watching, though not helping, my father tinker with what Mr Platard had come to call 'his latest'; and I left him to his tinkering and walked down the hill to the creek.

Already the creek had returned to its banks, though there was debris among the blackberry bushes and along the banks, and in the paddocks, tussocks and clumps of rushes were bent low. I walked upstream from the bridge until I saw the silhouette of a man striding a rise under a low slateheap of cloud that threatened rain.

When I reached the rise, the man was standing back from the bank, casting into the stream. He cast upstream, drew in line as it drifted toward him, then with quick movement of rod lifted the line from the water, moved two paces along the bank, and cast again. There were three trout hanging below his belt.

I had never seen anyone fish like that before. My own fishing had been with a handline and worms, and I had caught blackfish that were dark and as slippery as eels. Many had been too small to be worth taking home, and these I had cut loose and watched as they darted beneath a bank or among reeds. In summer months when the pools were bright and transparent, I had often watched trout feeding and playing, yet only once had I caught one. I had set a line overnight, and in the morning pulled from the water a small trout, its gills barely moving. I returned him to the water where he jerked about off-balance, in the shallows. Later I saw him, floating, white underbelly up and pink gills flared wide; and I had not fished with set lines again.

'Hey kid!'

The fisherman was motioning to me with the landing net.

'Hey kid, come 'n hold this.'

I carried the net for him, and watched the movements his wrist made in lifting and casting; and I thought of my father's big hands at work with a hammer, tin-snips and soldering iron.

No other fish had fallen to his sunken flies when it began to rain. We hurried across tussocks toward his truck, then I asked him to our house and we changed direction. He was a big man, taller than my father, though thick at the waist like Mr Platard, and he huffed with the exertion of hurrying up the muddy rise to the house.

In the kitchen, the fisherman and I stood in our socks and warmed ourselves with our backs to the stove and with steaming mugs of tea that my mother poured. The fisherman introduced himself and laid his trout on the table in front of my father and Mr Platard. He said they were not bad for such a small stream, though he was used to getting among the big 'uns.

'Like Sat'day 'fore last. Out on Burrumbeat with Ed Dyson. Trout rose twenty yards out. Four poun' I sez t' Ed. I cast over him with a Red Tag . . . He went four poun' orright.'

The fisherman's stories began to follow each other in procession. In all of them the fish were huge and his casting true and victorious.

During a pause between stories I told him of a big trout in a pool below the bridge, just near where he left his truck. The fisherman said he doubted there'd be one there 'cause of traffic over the bridge. I said the trout had been there two years, at least, and in summer, when the creek cleared, I'd show him. The fisherman said he'd sure like to see this whale of mine.

And it was summer, with the creek running bright and clear, before the fisherman came again.

During that time my father converted two of the chicken pens into drying sheds, with rows of racks on which the clay was to be spread, and he worked on the motor and crusher until they were at least functioning, the two of them belted together, vibrating on their mountings and making a great racket while the beaters inside flayed around and around. He was going to prepare clay for fine pottery, he said. Some of the clay at the pit was white kaolin of top quality. But it had to be treated right. It had to be dried and then crushed, dried further and crushed further until it was as smooth as talcum. Then he'd bag it and send it by train all around the country. There were groups of people all over producing fine pottery, he said. Pottery was a coming thing. Things would work out this time. This time things were sure to work out right.

When the fisherman saw the trout he said he'd nail him for sure.

Summer had turned the creek into separate pools linked by a thin strand of water tinkling over gravel. With the pools now clear, the fisherman used a floating fly. He would cast to the head of a pool, and the fly would drift slowly toward us on the slack current. Three times there had been a sudden breaking of surface, the flash of sunlight on back, an abrupt tightening of line. The rod had jerked and bowed and vibrated. Once, rod and line had gone suddenly slack, and the fisherman cursed the fish that escaped him.

So, holding the landing net and two fish, I showed the fisherman the big trout. We were standing on the bridge with the pool spreading out below us, before it narrowed into a tail confined between dark rocks. But where it was wide and shallow there were clumps of rushes, and in their shadow lay the trout.

In a river or a lake a three-pound trout is considered a good fish; but in a small stream, a fish that size is accounted a monster.

As we watched, a white cabbage-moth flew over the pool. The trout made an abrupt movement, then lay straight and stiff but for the agitated fanning of tail. The moth fluttered low, then began to rise again. There was a rush through water, the fish leaping high in air, plucking moth from its flight. The trout splashed back into the pool with corrugation after corrugation disturbing the surface. I hoisted myself to the railing of the bridge to see better, and saw the trout dart back to the cover of the rushes. The fisherman said there was no hope of getting him that day, now he'd been scared.

'But I'll be back,' he said. 'I'll be back t' nail him. I'll nail him f' sure.'

My father's preparations of clay for pottery proceeded, beneath the mocking gazes of my mother, Mr Platard and myself. He must have become aware of our attitude, for among us he was often moodily silent. But right through the long and hot summer days he worked with a kind of dreamy pleasure, grubbing out white clay from among seams of yellow, spreading white clods on the racks, raking over drying clay, feeling the powdery texture of clay that had been crushed. There were days when the crusher rattled and vibrated from early morning until dark, and days of north winds when he opened out the ends of the sheds to funnel the hot, drying winds over the racks.

Long before summer was over he was shovelling powdered clay into heavy-duty bags, and trucking them to the railway station.

Sometimes his truck broke down and he had to spend days working on it. But though he complained about the cost of truck parts and of freight, he kept telling my mother that things would work out this time. He was getting a return on the work already; he was sure things would work out this time.

It was summer, the weather not yet broken, when the fisherman next came. He drove right up to the house and announced he'd nail that whale of mine that day.

Even my father knocked off work to watch. The fisherman ushered us all down to a spot below the pool, explaining we would have to come up to the pool from down-stream so as not to disturb the trout. He showed us from where we could watch, and set up his rod and reel, greasing the line and the fine leader before tying on the fly. Then he crawled to the dark rocks at the tail of the pool.

Kneeling, he began working the line in the air, whipping it back and forth along the length of the pool, not allowing it to touch the surface, but shooting out line until it was curving through the air beyond the rushes. The fly and line were brought gently to the surface; leader, line and rod forming a line on the glassy surface, straight from fly to fisherman.

From where the four of us watched, the pool, the fisherman, and the fly all seemed motionless. Then there was a movement in the water beyond the fly, a sudden sucking sound and the fly was gone, the line taut, the rod bowed and swinging from side to side as the line cut wide arcs in the pool. The surface erupted in a fury of splashing, and the rod was alive with jerkings and vibrations, the fisherman reeling in, letting out line, working the rod against the fish's straining, then reeling in more surely, the fish deep down and closer in, the rod and line swinging in smaller arcs, then the rod bowed like a hair pin but no longer swinging, the line almost perpendicular and the fisherman reaching for the landing net. Holding the rod at arm's length behind him he reached with the net down into the water. He began to raise the net. There was a sudden breaking of surface, drag-out of line, the rod wrenched into an inverted U, then rebounding in sudden release.

My father was the first to realize what had happened. He jumped down the bank and ran to the fisherman.

'That was a great go,' he said. 'Great go. Guess it's the best I've seen.'

I followed my mother and Mr Platard down the bank to the fisherman. My father kept saying what a great 'go' it had been, but my mother and Mr Platard both said what a disappointment that the trout had got away.

My father picked up the fisherman's bag and rod, I folded the landing net, and we carried them for him as we climbed the bank and the rise to the house, my father a little in front. The fisherman dawdled behind, then ran and caught up. He'd nail that trout next time, he said. There'd be no getting away next time 'cause he'd sure make sure he nailed him then.

Before the following week was out, the rains came. After a week of steady rain the creek swirled clay-yellow and clay-white. It was still raining and we had not seen the fisherman again, when the trout season ended.

The change in weather brought a change to my father's business. The truck would lumber out the sodden drive at first light, to return at dusk with white ooze running out from between the boards of its wooden tray. My father's boots and clothes would be soaked, caked and smeared in white, his hands blue with cold. And now that sun-heat and wind-heat no longer dried the clay, days were spent carting wood. In each shed he built a fireplace with a system of ducting air through the racks. Fires had to be kept burning day and night. Sometimes a week passed without sufficient clay for a crushing.

At night my father began constructing columns of figures down the margins of newspapers. He would check off the items in the column, add it up, then scribble over it and begin another.

By mid winter more and more days were spent working on the truck, and less and less bags of powdered clay were delivered to the train.

One day Mr Platard told my father to add water to the clay after it was crushed so it would weigh heavier and he would be paid more; but my father shook his head at this. Later, Mr Platard had another idea. It was that my father just might have some show of not falling flat again, if he had someone else dig out the clay while he attended to the truck, the racks, and the crusher. My father nodded at this. But when Mr Platard named men out of work who would jump at any job, my father said rain had made the pit dangerous — sides had slipped and caved in — and it wasn't right to ask anyone else to work there. Mr Platard guffawed and said it was going to be the chicken business all over again.

The year had again progressed to the trout season, to days of rain alternating with days of spring heat, when the fisherman came again. My father returned with a load of wood and told me he had seen the fisherman's truck just up from the bridge. He asked me to help him unload, but I said the fisherman got what *he* was after, and walked down the road to the bridge. The fisherman was not at his truck, nor was he along the banks. I heard a gunshot from the hill behind the creek. Later I heard three more shosts. When I returned to the bridge the truck was gone.

The next weekend I saw the rabbit beneath the

bridge. It had been partly skinned and flies were crawling over the exposed parts. As I watched, a maggot dropped from the rabbit and sank as it was carried through the pool. I stood looking at the drab yellow-brown water, and wondered if the trout had stayed at the pool through the winter.

A week later, a day of brown and grey, the fisherman came to the house.

By then my father's truck had broken down beyond all repair, Mr Platard had loaded the last of the bags of clay into his latest car — another Chev, with twin-speaker wireless and carpets — and taken them to the railway. My father was again working at the council crusher.

The fisherman said there'd be no mistake about nailing the trout this time, and we all pulled on gumboots and followed him down the hill. He did not have his rod and bag, but carried only the landing net and a hank of heavy cord with a hook tied to one end.

We slithered and slipped along the muddy bank, and the fisherman went to a tree where another rabbit was hanging. He collected two maggosts from the carcass and threaded them onto the hook. Then he simply walked along the bank and threw the line into the head of the pool. At once he struck, and hand over hand dragged the trout from the water and up the bank. The trout thrashed in mud. The fisherman took a knife from his belt and pushed it through the trout's head and bent the body back against the knife until the neck broke.

Smiling, he held the trout up by the tail to show us.

'He's a good 'un, orright,' he said, coming over to us. 'A real good 'un. Just show y': there's more 'un one way.'

Mr Platard and my mother gathered around, congratulating him and hefting the weight of the trout. My father remained at a distance.

I followed the fisherman, Mr Platard, and my

mother up the rise, the fisherman holding the trout up in front of him by the gills. At the top of the rise he called back to me:

'Hey kid! Get the net an' knife, will y'?'

Slithering back down the bank, I landed on my knees in the mud. I saw my father still standing by the dark rocks.

'He shouldn't have got him that way,' I said, walking up to him.

'No,' my father said, 'He shouldn't have.'

We stood there silently, looking at the pool. The fisherman called for his net and knife.

I did not answer. I looked down at the dark rocks and heard my mother call to me, asking was I, for God's sake, going to turn moody like my father?

Then the fisherman gave the fish to Mr Platard and clambered down the rise to the knife and the net. Mr Platard and my mother stood looking at me. Mr Platard pronounced their disappointment: they had thought I was the boy who'd learnt a thing or two!

My father and I watched the three of them set off toward the house. Someone laughed.

I said I guessed the fisherman didn't have what it took, though I was not sure if my meaning was clear.

However my father must have apprehended my meaning. He grinned. Nodded and grinned, seemed momentarily young and gay, and skipped a stone across the pool.

We scrambled up the slippery rise and walked, together, across paddocks, past the broken-down trucks, the heaps of rusting iron and the empty sheds.

Mime With Fox and Hawk

Long before strudel and coffee, she (on my left) and he (on my right) abandoned even those where-did-you-go-last-holiday questions and sat, just sat, digestive juices at work, eyes in blank unfocus at the rain.

I might, you say, at least have tried?

I did. I did. I was all question-then-listen-intently during bean soup with sour cream, I was expansive over goulash on rice; it was not till we returned from the hot smorgasboard that I withdrew from the Eden of piled plate and warm belly, of laugh-on-the-punchline stories. For then — at a table's separation from us — there occured a prelude to tragedy. At least, I apprehended it as such; and attempted to communicate the primality of the drama. 'You story-tellers', she (on my left) said, 'always making things up!' Earnestly I addressed her: 'Madam I do not invent, I observe, I select and interpret'. Then I glimpsed the smile I was intended not to glimpse. Humour him, the smile (on my right) urged, — we've been warned.

What, then, could I do — except reach for the wine bottle, then silently observe, select, and interpret?

And just what, you ask, was this vignette of drama?

Patience, patience. There is first the drama's décore to be arranged in your mind, sound and backdrop presented to the ears and eyes of your imagination.

Within a log-cabin restaurant, allow your imagination a place at table. Facing the door, to left a log fire then hot and cold smorgasboard beneath threaded loops of dried chillies. To right, windows are intended to exhibit mountain ash and stringy-bark ranges, but, remember? it is raining. Rain hangs as a trans-luscent, eighty-degree-striated, curtain.

There remains the backdrop. Occupying an entire wall, buffet to door, hip-height to ceiling, is an atrociously executed mural. There a sky of dense and unvarying blue descends to breast-shaped hills with dead-centre cleavage that are a dense and unvarying green; beside a tree, a fox leaps (if it *is* a fox, with shoulders and haunches as muscular as a boxer's). The fox leaps beside its young, above which a hawk hovers. The depiction appears to lack logic, for the hawk — talons extended, small neat body suspended on fragile wings — appears no match at all for the muscular leaping fox or its replica-in-reduced-size young. Yet the leaps of fox and pup are leaps of anguish, and the hawk's talons drip gore.

With rain drubbing a drum-roll on the iron roof, the performers arrive. By stationwagon. Pulling in close under the eaves. Then spills in through the doorway, him and her, his and hers, and theirs.

Him: less than forty, more than six feet, affecting a cravat and suede jacket, spreading down and out from chest to waist and much aware of it, for this is a physique whose achievements once were cheered by thousands.

For what, you ask?

Not track and field (the back too, too, wide); not boxing (nasal bridge still intact); not wrestling, not rugby (no cauliflowers blossom on those ears); yet football, yes; Australian Rules, yes, yes.

You say this is mere speculation?

This, reader, is observation. Observation plus deduction. I have observed, for instance, the company name on the stationwagon door. From this I deduce that football fame had eased the step from company rep, to area-manager; his abilities, however, limited, he remains a manager who is managed.

His: at fifteen, the son is high though knobbly with bone as the frame waits to put on sheets and planks of muscle. In noting strength in the twin cords of muscle bordering the throat, one gleans this is a son whose spring and summer evenings are spent in a gym, whose autumn and winter after-school steps take him, running, to a football field. In the son's turn-of-head and gaze to father, one sees no mere mateyness or camaraderie: one sees worship. Oh yes-s-s, and the son, image of the father and Anglo-Celt Australian to the last nerve and sinew, contains not a single one of her Oriental genes and chromosomes.

Her: while observation can present his life to me (Australian myself, ex-bikey myself) as fully scripted as if viewed on a twenty-four inch screen, the minutiae of her life is beyond my deductions. I observe merely a tiny but proportioned body clothed in the discreet sophistication of open crocheted poncho over black; I see her coiffure perfect in its blackness, perfect in its absence of whisps or strays, nails honed to ten perfect cloisters where no chip mars the paintwork.

Hers: at eleven or twelve, not a pretty child. Yet some instinct announces she will by-pass prettiness to be moulded by her mother to beauty. Also, there are no more of his Anglo-Celt genes in the wife's daughter, than there are her Oriental genes in the husband's son.

Theirs: twin boys where his weight of bone combines with the gleaming black of her hair to produce these cute-as-dolls three-year-olds in tartan jackets and red bow ties.

The husband has indicated a table. Instantly his wife's daughter, twin in each hand, assumes lead. She arranges twins at table on one side, herself central opposite. Wife has crossed in front of husband to sit next to the twins. There remains for father and son only those places at the most disadvantageous position *vis-a-vis* each other: on the same side but separated by the step-daughter step-sister. In the father's frozen stare to roof-beams, in the son's glance to father, glare to step-sister to step-mother, is realization they have been subjects of a manoeuvre; in the infinitessimal nod, mother to daughter, is reward.

On to her husband's frozen stare, the wife now switches on and directs the radiator of her smile. She holds the menu at the calculated-to-a-degree angle that lures his gaze to hers, where, thawing, it gives back a watery reflection of her smile.

Without moving her smiling gaze, the wife tosses an order to the waitress standing pad-poised beside her. The order is so brief it can only be drinks for the children. While the waitress retreats, then advances with orangeade for the children, son leans across table (as he must) in futile attempt to draw his father's attention to him. Wife snares husband's attention with indications of this, on the menu, and that, or, should he prefer it, that . . .

Aha, you say, a wicked step-mother is villain of the piece.

Not here a heroine as sweet, as unblemished, as untouched by life as an unlicked ice-cream, a villain so coated with life's soot as to be fit only to be hissed, booed, and pelted with pop-corn.

The lady is from islands teeming and off-shore from a teeming continent, where war, occupation, and mouths by the million, have catapulted its people into fifty-to-a-bench assembly lines, into smog, into fifteen-story seven-to-a-room apartments, into hostess bars to become items on expense accounts. Having escaped, do you wonder she should use beauty, use guile, to put from her what she regards as a threat.

Consider, as the waitress brings coffee, brings cakes, the threat. Consider, and calculate: the father aged, say, thirty-nine; from this subtract the son's age, allow for pre- or post-marital conception, now calculate the father's age at first marriage. The answer is . . . an age at which one does not marry for position, for money, nor (if one is a football hero) for companionship or sex alone. Whether hopelessly romantic, whether booted from back-seat copulations to altar-front vows, whether long- or short-lived, — one marries for love. To love add the peculiarly southern Australian obsession with football, and doubt not the babe was still in bassinet when first taken to the very fence-front row of benches.

As the Church states a child theirs till seven is theirs for life; so this child till, perhaps, seven, had mud-covered and bruised players as his saints and apostles, whiff from bar and hot-dog stand his incense, game from ball-bounce to siren-blast the enactment of ritual. And seeing his father lifted to shoulders to be cheered and run-after and cheered with hoarse-throated adulation, was to see the transformation of man into a god.

The wife — present wife — no doubt accepts her husband has in his son a link with another time, another wife. But more, much more, than that. For the father, his frame now spreading, his fame now thinning, the sound of remembered cheering becoming faint in his mind's ear, sees his son's frame growing, his son's fame beginning, the sound of cheering already sporadically heard, and he, the object of worship, begins himself to worship.

The relationship from worshiper to worshipee is one from which non-worshipers are excluded: history is comma'd and colon'd with the neglects of worshipers.

While the wife holds in snare her husband's gaze, she daintily eats cake with a fork. Orangeade is syphoned from three glasses, and stays unsyphoned in a fourth. Beneath smiles, beneath words, the wife's glance checks and checks that orangeade level. Waiting no longer, she addresses words and gestures to hers and theirs and, most emphatically, his, then indicates the wide and dripping eaves outside. No parade-ground bellow could be reacted to more instantaneously than this is by the daughter. She stands, gathers twins, crosses between tables, takes from stationwagon a ball and initiates a ball game beneath the eaves.

The youth remains. His father's wife repeats the gesture to the eaves outside. She turns to husband. Earnestly she entreats. The son interrupts. At the son's voice the father reacts with instant head-turn and smile. The smile fades, and when the youth again speaks, his father gives an unsmiling nod. Though the nod has a she'll-be-right-label, the son doubts content — for still he makes no move. The father stirs coffee, taps a spoon, stirs. Watching him, his wife ceases her entreaties; watching him, the son remains.

This impasse is broken by the son. He stands. At a single gulp he tosses off the orangeade. He passes between tables, through door, takes from the stationwagon (you still think this mere speculation?) a football. Beneath eaves he bounces the ball once, twice, then hugs ball to chest as he stands back-to-window. He stares through rain.

Inside, colour-tipped hands gesture, colour-tinged muscles at cheek and temple first bunch then extend, to invoke the severance of the son from the family unit. Details of plot, whether boarding school, army apprenticeship, navy cadetship, life with friend in country or uncle interstate, are overlayed by the tramp of rain on roof. What is open to all gazes is the wife leaning forward in the intensity of her entreaties, the father racked between decision and decision, and the son waiting.

Slowly, the wife leans back. She selects, taps, lights a cigarette, exhales a long high plume of smoke. As though an after thought, she gives another of her infinitesimal nods.

No whisp of smoke proclaiming the election of a pope could be more avidly awaited than this by the daughter. She gathers twins, ushers them to door, jollies them to stand heels together, straight, and smiling.

Husband and wife are rising, are crossing to waitress and cash-register. From the effusive waitress, husband turns — to see his son entering at the door, crossing toward him, stopping in front of the mural.

Wife impassively crosses in front of her husband's son, then her impassivity breaks as she clasps daughter, clasps twins, as she gives what-good-children pats and hugs.

Father moves to son. He reaches a hand toward a shoulder that is instantly withdrawn beyond reach of his touch. The hand stays raised ridiculously, as the son emits a single, high, gasping cry: the sound an animal might make in feeling talons rip through pelt and flesh and into guts.

The father stands in a suspended gesture of touching. Son backs through door, turns, runs beyond eaves to stand shrouded in rain.

At the cry, eyes in the room have turned. Eyes stare at the oddness of the father's stance. All eyes stare, except mine. I observe no more. How long youth stands in rain, how long man stands before mural, I know only from hearing laughter at first suppressed to giggles, become unrestrained and raucous.

When I do look, there is only the mural. The atrociously inept depiction of the mural.

At least, you say, smiling, that artist did better than a certain storyteller who puffed these paragraphs to inflate a rabbit-mound into an Everest.

Reader, mock if you will my inadequate art. But for those of whom I have told, I implore your pity: her talons, dear reader, her talons were red.

Mister Al

Al McCurdy was thirty when the notion took root and grew in him that he would gamble all or nothing to change his life.

He had been born into what, in the late 1940's, was the last Victorian township supported by gold.

There was no pub, no railway, no shop or police-station; but Carey's place was also the Post Office, and there was a school.

It was a school with no library, no craft room, no quadrangle, no basketball courts. The school possessed one football and a paddock with pine trees for goal posts at one end, gum trees at the other.

Yet this school was the envy of schools that were cluttered with sports equipment and teaching aids, that had craft and music and sports teachers and twenty times the number of pupils. This school had Allen.

For at the once-a-year inter-school sports, Allen won. Won — the first year he was old enough to compete — both events in which he could compete. Next year he again won the 50 yards and the 100 yards — and the 200 yards too. The year after, it was the 50, 100, 200, 400; and the year after added the long jump as well.

The entire school travelled the thirty-odd miles to these triumphs. Mine shift workers who were 'off' came too, bringing their wives and the wives of mine shift workers who were 'on'. Even Carey's did what they were forbidden to do — closed the post office for the day and came.

They came to cheer Al (already Allan had become Al), Al McCurdy. They all said he'd be a champ one day. He'd go to the Games. Too right he would!

He was fourteen when the mine closed and the McCurdy family moved to Melbourne. He began work as a turning and fitting improver.

Following his years as an improver, he stood each day at the same lathe, adjusting the flow of white coolant onto components for agricultural valves. These varied only in diameter, and on Tuesdays and Thursdays he machined casts of stems, while on Mondays, Wednesdays, Fridays, it was discs.

Having joined a suburban athletic club, Al McCurdy found he was one good runner — among many good runners.

During his first year, he won the club's 100 metre championship and was second in the 200 metre. He was unplaced over either distance in the State Championships.

That was the way it went as he outgrew junior ranks to compete in B Grade senior competition, then A Grade.

He played Association Football one winter and spring, in the seconds mostly, for the extra five pounds because he was getting married. Two months after the wedding he took Roslyn to hospital. There he learnt they would not be able to have children. As well as taking that aspiration, the hospital took all of those five pounds and much more; so that owning their own quarter-acre block and brick veneer home in an outer suburb became another aspiration denied them.

So they were stuck in the rented house which trams rattled past till forty-seven minutes past midnight every night. Trams going up the hill, causing the wireless to splutter with static; trams going down the hill to rattle plates against each other on cupboard shelves.

Those five pounds also caused him to be struck from running again as an amateur.

During his first season as a pro, he won two minor

Gifts at country sports carnivals. After that he was back to the 6 yard handicap mark in the Gift distance of 120; and during the following summers he won heats only, not finals.

Those he had won gained him only prize money. He did not bet. However training track gossip was rife with tales of those who brought off betting coups.

There was Rick Stringer the year he won at Echuca. Rick trained under Swampy Powell, and he ran the '55 season a full stone overweight and was reckoned to be over the hill and on a downhill slide. He started the next season just as heavy and just as slow. Handicapper Joe Guillet gave his handicap mark a two yard lift in '55, then another yard at the beginning of '56.

Rick Stringer didn't enter for any carnival for six weeks before Echuca, then turned up looking strong and fit and as lean as a greyhound.

Before the heats were run, Swampy Powell had his runners organized for a plunge on the bookies. That was the one way to get high odds — bet on the final before the heats were run.

Rick won, of course. Heat and final.

Handicapper Joe Guillet came to where Swampy Powell was counting money.

'You beat me this time. Beat me pointless.'

'What y' mean?' Swampy asked.

'Oh, innocent!' Joe Guillet said. 'As innocent as a swamp fox with a mouth full of chook feathers!'

Joe Guillet dragged Rick two and a half yards for his Echuca win. But that didn't matter. Rick had got two hundred on at between twenty- and eighty-to-one, and he paid cash for a house on a new subdivision and a new Holden car.

Al McCurdy went to Swampy. He said he wanted to set himself for one all-or-nothing plunge.

'It'll be a two-year program,' Swampy said. 'If y' do bring it off, Joe Guillet 'll drag yer handicap back so far — you'll never win another.'

Al McCurdy reckoned by that time he'd be thirty-two. Age would be waiting to drag him back harder than any handicapper.

'Awright,' Swampy said. 'But you'll need t' take a real tight grip o' y'self. What beats most that try this on, ain't other runners and it ain't the handicapper nor the bookies neither. It's themselves.'

Al McCurdy reckoned that standing at the same repetition lathe year after year, hearing trams rattle past the house till near one every night, his childless and insipid marriage — gave him all the motivation he'd ever need.

At the first carnival of the following season, Joe Guillet saw Al McCurdy among Swampy's runners.

'New boy, Swampy?'

'Old boy,' Swampy said. 'But it keeps him fit and out've the pub — y'know?'

'*I* know,' Joe Guillet said.

Al McCurdy was twelve pound heavier than ever he'd been. Steak and spuds, chops and spuds, and bananas — by the pound!

'Twelve poun', eh,' Swampy had said. 'Drink a bottle of beer every night till you're up a good stone and a half.'

This extra weight Swampy insisted he put on was really a precaution. Swampy had seen runners go to the blocks with every intention of running dead, then they had changed in that interminable second, second-and-a-half, two seconds, while their weight was forward on their fingertips.

They'd changed — not by making a decision — but in their legs, their belly, in the whole motor of their running. At the starter's gun they'd blasted out of the blocks and twelve seconds later been astounded to find they'd breasted the tape first — and blown their one chance to set themselves up for life.

Swampy laid it down to Al McCurdy that runners are either natural drivers or natural floaters. Drivers got the most from their greater strength by driving fast out from the blocks. Floaters ran like a rooster, clawing the track. They rarely had the strength for an explosive start. So there was always one place a floater could improve a yard or more — at the start. Al McCurdy was a floater.

So instead of pre-season jogging and stretching exercises, throughout winter and spring Al McCurdy had worked out in a gymnasium. With increasing weights he did squats, half-squats, jump-squats. He did arm exercises of bench presses and punching a heavy bag. Swampy was emphatic about the bench presses and the punching — to get out of the blocks fast, arms have to become pistons that drive the legs.

He kept up the gymnasium work through the summer, though now he did sprint training as well. He stopped training with other pro runners. Instead he went alone to a football oval a mile from where he lived.

There were drab houses on three sides of the oval; on the other, the hill side, was a council park crowned with a memorial to fallen soldiers. Oaks and maples spread and shed their leaves over the slope where a path curved down in a wide swooping curve.

Al McCurdy had run four seventy-yard run-throughs, when he heard a delirious yell. He looked up to see three boys on bikes, one in a billy cart, hurtling down the path.

He yelled too — sure the four would crash into the iron rail surrounding the oval. Without braking, two swerved their bikes right, one left, and the billy cart shot straight beneath the rail, out across the oval.

Twice more the boys performed their delirious downhill career. Then they tired of the game, and watched him.

They began waiting for him each Tuesday and

Thursday. Soon he had the boys time him. Then he was conducting races for them. When Lenny, the biggest, won every race, he introduced a handicap system. This enabled Snow, the smallest, the first time in his life to win a race. After that Snow looked upon Mister Al as toward one at whose command oceans would part.

Al McCurdy ran at all of that summer's carnivals without winning a heat. Joe Guillet lifted his handicap mark from 6 yards to 7, then at Stawell he was out to 8.

When the season was over, he went straight to increasing his work at the gym. Not till September did he go to the footy oval.

Swampy Powell had started a new bank account of his own. That was the way Swampy operated — he built up a separate account for each runner in his stable. On the day for which that runner was set, he'd empty the account in one plunge on the bookies.

Roslyn had begun taking an interest in Al's running she hadn't taken since early marriage. She had a screw-top jar into which she put coins, even notes, saved from her housekeeping. That was her lounge-suite money, she said. If the odds were real good, a new fridge too. For their new house.

On Sunday afternoons Al and Roslyn McCurdy drove beyond the tram tracks to where a grid of macadam streets and concrete curbing were imposed on what had been a cherry orchard. Or they parked behind other cars outside a display home, to enter where a man was talking and talking while expansively opening doors onto rooms and cupboards.

Roslyn took all of the plans and the pamphlets she was offered. She kept these in a Weetie packet. When she took out all the pamphlets and plans to spread them across the kitchen table, she even turned off the wireless.

Al McCurdy's own dream went beyond a brick

veneer house in a new housing estate. It included a truck that would take him away from the agricultural valve factory, out along the road to Shepparton for a load of apples and pears, or coming down from Mildura with oranges, or carting beef-on-the-hoof with road and countryside and sky open and wide all the way from Bourke to Newmarket.

When country sports carnivals began in November, he knew he had the strength to drive hard and fast out from the blocks. But he ran dead; and Joe Guillet gave his handicap mark another yard lift.

His bank account had advanced past two hundred when in Christmas week Swampy said:

'Bendigo Gift. March 10.'

With the agricultural valve factory closed for Christmas holidays, Al McCurdy trained twice a day. Jogging and exercises in the mornings, track work at the footy oval each afternoon. Fruit and black tea became his breakfast, cheese and salad his lunch, fish and salad his dinner. And Snow, holding the stopwatch, looked at where the hands had stopped to exclaim, 'Gee-*ee*!'

Other kids were there too, of course. Often he had thirty, at times thirty-six, thirty-seven, for whom he conducted races.

One day he looked along the line of kids he was trying to prevent cribbing forward on their handicap marks, to see Roslyn standing beside a goal post. For the last race of that day, it was she who clapped her hands in imitation of a starter's pistol.

By then Al McCurdy was back at the factory. He was also training an hour and a half before work, then going straight from work to the footy oval.

One Sunday morning Swampy came to where Mister Al was organizing races. Without telling the kids, he fired a starter's pistol. He did that twice more.

Then the joke was over and he called Al McCurdy over.

'Joe Guillet's heard you're a stone and a half down an' it's no great deduction you're set t' fly. So you better have a couple of runs before Bendigo. Run terrible. Or he'll be right onto you.'

When Joe Guillet saw Al McCurdy at Ballarat, he said:

'Your boy's fined down, Swampy.'

'Been crook,' Swampy said. 'Shouldn't be runnin' as much as t' the corner shop for a 'paper. Had diarrhoea somethin' shocking.'

Alone with Al McCurdy, Swampy said: 'Fall over.'

When Swampy saw Al McCurdy rocket out of the blocks, his mouth gaped open. He did not close it for six seconds. That is, until half way down the track and leading, Al McCurdy pitched forward to sprawl his length on the track.

The week before Bendigo, Al McCurdy was entered for Lilydale.

As he crossed the car park, he saw faded letters across the sides of a dry cleaner's delivery van. He recalled seeing those letters somewhere . . . Then he saw the kids clustered among the crowd near the start. There were fifteen, twenty, perhaps more. And among them a woman worriedly jabbed at kids to 'Siddown!', and 'Don't you go 'way!', and 'If I lose you in this crowd what'll your mum think o' *me*?'

He went to the change room and did warm-up exercises. When his heat of the Gift was called, he took his blocks to the start.

'Mister Al!' the kids chorused. 'Mister Al!'

Without looking at them, he waved. At the starter's bark, he went into his blocks. He looked straight at the tape across his lane 120 yards away. Yet though he could keep the chorusing kids out of his sight, he could not keep them out of his awareness.

The gun boomed — and he drove at the blocks as

he glimpsed Snow's mouth open in a cheer. He still seemed to see that open mouth as his mind said, Slow down! — and then to yell, Slow! Slow!

He tried to slow and pitched forward. He was falling when he broke through the tape.

He regained his feet, realizing as he did that Rick Stringer's younger brother Clarry, had just pipped him.

Returning his lane colour to the official table, he jogged across to the kids.

Snow said: 'This's me Mum.'

'This whole thunderin' herd I've gotta look after on me own,' she said. 'An' you don't even win.'

'He would've,' one kid shouted. 'Only he tripped.'

'That one in blue,' one said. '*He* should've tripped!'

Lenny said: 'I reckon you *was* first!'

'Yair-*air*!' Snow shouted. 'All them judges 're crooks!'

'He beat me,' Mister Al said. 'Too right he did.'

Just then the Gift finalists were announced and he, not listening, was startled by the kids all cheering. He snatched the program off Snow's mother. There was confirmed: heat winners and fastest second went into the final.

Snow's mother said: 'P'rhaps me day won't be wasted.'

In the change room, Clarry Stringer was running on the spot in his track suit.

'First Gift Final?' Al McCurdy asked.

'Yair,' Clarry Stringer said. 'The first.'

Al McCurdy wished him luck.

'You're the one t' beat,' Clarry Stringer said.

'Keep Ray Boer in y' sights,' Al McCurdy said. 'Don't you worry about me.'

Clarry Stringer stopped running on the spot. It might be his first season running as a pro, but he would know with Bendigo, Wangaratta, Stawell coming up, any runner who'd set himself for one of the big ones wouldn't want to blow his mark at Lilydale.

'Thanks,' Clarry Stringer said, grinning, beginning to run on the spot again. 'Gee, thanks.'

Al McCurdy went to where Swampy and his other runners sat on the grass inside the track.

'This time don't leave it so late to pull up,' Swampy said. 'You'll pull a hamstring.'

At the official table, Joe Guillet gave him his lane colour.

'Yer first final in years,' Joe Guillet said. 'An' you a sick man!'

While the two-mile was being run, Al McCurdy set up his blocks. He glanced once at the kids and saw Snow's dad, holding a glass and unsteady on his feet, among them now.

Too soon the public address system was naming the runners, and each in turn waved to the crowd as he ran half way down the track and back. It was then Al McCurdy felt what in four years he had not felt — tension knotted like wind in his belly.

'On yer marks!'

In abrupt silence, the eight finalists stepped into their blocks. A solitary girl's voice called: 'Carn Mister Al!' Then like a chorused litany: 'Yair-*air*!'

'Get set!'

His weight forward on his fingertips, Al McCurdy realized his arms were shaking. He shifted weight on his fingertips. The shaking would not stop.

Just then Clarry Stringer broke. The gun boomed — twice — and the rest jogged along the track then back to behind their blocks. At the starter's first bark, the finalists again went into their blocks.

'Get set!'

No matter how he altered weight on his fingertips, his arms shook and shook. There was no sound except his own breathing, and he glanced around as though he expected to find the other runners and the entire sports ground of spectators all gone home. But there they were, the kids, the care-worn woman, the man holding a glass, all in postures as unnaturally immobile as his own.

The gun boomed. Al McCurdy felt caught unawares and he drove, drove hard, driving the blocks behind him, his arms punching like pistons to drive the legs.

He had not heard the crowd's roar and certainly not the shouted cheer of kids. But his legs, his belly, his arms punching like pistons knew — knew the cheer of kids from as far back as inter-school sports, kids cheering who'd had few victories of their own to cheer and adults with even fewer victories behind them and less chance of a victory ahead — cheering to make his victory their own.

And he was running, clawing the track behind him, as his mind screamed, Slow! Stumble!, and then, Trip! — Fall! — Fall! — Fall!

He was still running as he went through the tape. Then his body did obey his mind's command and he fell. He rolled and a runner coming behind jumped high to avoid spiking him.

He sat up as runners came to clap his back and shake his hand.

Though not Clarry Stringer.

'You tell me t' watch Ray Boer!'

The public address system announced placings and times.

'Yer time!' Clarry Stringer shouted a laugh of gleeful vindictiveness. 'Man! — will Joe Guillet crucify you!'

Joe Guillet looked as though he might too. Right there and then, as he crossed the grass toward them. But with a publicly expansive gesture, he thrust out his hand. Gripping Al McCurdy's hand, he pulled him in close.

'You beat me bloody pointless!'

Joe Guillet began ushering him toward the platform and the microphones there.

'I had you figured set f' Bendigo.'

'I wasn't set,' Al McCurdy said. 'Not a penny.'

'Tell me another!'

'I wasn't. Not a solitary shilling!'

'Listen, I don't care if you bled the bookies white. But *I* had a whole bank account set to empty on you at Bendigo!'

Then Al McCurdy was on the platform, a red sash across his shoulder, and the Mayor of Lilydale shaking his hand while presenting the cheque. Al McCurdy made a speech into the microphones. He remembered to thank the mayor and the organizing committee and the other runners and the spectators. He even made a joke — he thanked the bookies.

While others on the platform were laughing, he glanced down at the cheque — at the one and the two noughts — and he thought, *That's it, then. That's all.*

When he ran his victory lap, Swampy had his back to him. But as he ran toward the kids they surged out onto the oval, carrying forward on their surge the woman and the man holding a glass: *their* victory whole, glorious and without regret.

Already he was thinking of Roslyn — Roslyn with her screw-top jar and her Weetie packet of plans. He was thinking of Swampy.

When his lap was over, he went to Swampy.

'The kids -' he began.

Then Swampy exploded. The sounds of that explosion were to reverberate down his memory, though not at all in the way the sounds were intended.

The money he had won together with what was in the bank account, did buy a new lounge suite. There was enough over for the deposit on a 'fridge, and a week's holiday in Sydney.

Then it was back to five days each week adjusting white coolant on shafts and discs of agricultural valves, back to the house where trams rattled past till

1.47 every night. Though there came a change to that rented house that was greater than a new lounge suite and a 'fridge on HP.

Though Mister Al no longer trained, he continued going to the footy oval. Roslyn went there too. She now went as often as he, taking a plastic container of cordial and cups for the kids. If they — the kids — never did become sure whether some prank or what they said would fetch a cuff from Missus Al or whether she would hug them to her, they did come to know that house as the one where they should open the door and walk straight in. That was what was expected.

In time those who were no longer kids brought girlfriends, boyfriends, then wives and husbands and kids of their own.

'Kids!'

Al McCurdy was always to remember the sounds of Swampy Powell's explosion. 'That's what you ought t' stick to — kids!'

The Note Pad

After eleven years of marriage, Naylor's wife had left him. Her diminutive size beside him at branch-manager functions, had emphasised his own height and bulk, and her demure smile had been the springboard from which he dived into pleasantries with visiting state-managers and their wives, department heads, his own supervisor, state-manager, and respective wives.

The trouble with Joyce (as he thought of it) had commenced after her mother's death. At first he allowed for that and was patient with her; but as she returned and returned to resurrect what had once been buried between them, he at last cleared his throat and spoke in firmer tones. He reminded her it had been *their* decision, not his alone. She must surely see how difficult a change at this late stage would be. She agreed it would be difficult; and commenced visiting art galleries. He thought there might be advantages in such an interest; but at the next branch-managers' function she refused even to speak to the state manager's wife. She refused also her usual well-diluted Pimms and ordered Pernod instead. After three Pernods she slumped in one chair, propped feet on another, and demanded to be fed. A waiter brought biscuits on which were scattered pink globules of caviar. She said she wanted to *eat*, not nibble. She fancied . . . wel-l-l, fish-'n'-chips f' starters. A hu-u-u-uge pile of fish-'n'-chips wrapped in newspaper.

Four weeks later Joyce left him to live with a seldom-exhibited and little-known artist. She was going, she said (with a vulgarity that shocked him), to start pushing out babies while she was still able.

No company disadvantage came to Naylor from his unpartnered state. Indeed, those who had witnessed the Pernod-and-feed-me episode assumed it had been he who had left her and attributed to him considerable firmness of character. Besides, his state manager had himself divorced, then married his secretary of many years, the efficient, if juiceless and brittle, former Miss Motts.

No Miss Motts lay within Naylor's orbit; and therein loomed his problem, for he was inept at looking after himself.

It was this that caused him first to regret his firmness with Joyce, then to leave the bay-windowed and oak-surrounded house. The flat he moved to was quite new; and on his first night there he had slept and not-slept on the lounge carpet.

For much of the night he lay staring at the farther wall. Light from a streetlamp below divided the bare rectangle of wall into a triangle of light above and a triangle of dark below. His own life was as barren and as divided as that wall. The light part (more than ever since Joyce had left him) was filled with frenetic bustle; while from a dark and subterranean part came the cry he was lonely, lonely, lonely.

The cries came to him so clamorously that he padded across carpet to the kitchenette and the fridge. There was only another tin of sardines to the one he had eaten on arriving, so he ate from that and drank coffee. Then he set himself firmly to practical considerations.

His drip-dry shirts had not yet dripped dry; should he, then, leave for work wearing a damp clean shirt or an unwashed dry one? Of late these non-iron shirts, he recalled, had *looked* non-ironed — but how did you iron a shirt? Then there was the problem of furnishing the flat.

Next day, a catalogue in one hand and telephone in the other, Naylor solved the problem of furnishing.

The solution to his other problem took many telephone calls. At last an employment agency answered, yes, they had an entry on their books they were sure would prove just what he was looking for — could he leave a duplicate of the flat's key at the agency next morning?

The agency gave him the woman's name, though no mention of whether she was Miss, Mrs, or Ms. Naylor solved the problem of how to address and communicate by purchasing a note pad and writing, thus:

> G.D.
> Goodmorning.
> Clean flat, wash and iron shirts buy breakfast foods from $10 in drawer. Buy something for lounge wall — not a print — perhaps one of those geometric thread and nail things. Buy from $30 in drawer.
>
> M.N.

That evening Naylor was confronted by a large spirograph that hung central in the previously bare wall. Its design of pretentious artiness was without any of the possibly disturbing suggestiveness of reproduced art. On the notepad was written:

> M.N.
> Goodevening.
> Spirograph cost $25.50, receipt and $4.50 change in drawer. Food bought. Supermarket checkout slip for $9.75 and .25c change in drawer. Will darn socks tomorrow. Also turn shirt cuffs. You need hankies.
>
> G.D.
>
> P.S. Do you prefer middle rashes or streaky bacon?

Naylor had not the least idea. He was so surprised at G.D.'s stated intention to perform such unasked-for, such very *personal*, services for him as darn socks and turn cuffs, that next morning he wrote:

Dear G.D.
Goodmorning.
Please clean flat, wash and iron shirts . . . etc.

That evening the note pad read:

Dear M.N.
Goodevening.
Your hankies cost $3.40. If eating alone at home, I can have a simple meal ready for you; if entertaining I can prepare something more elaborate that you will only have to turn a knob to cook or reheat. Veal dishes — such as Parmigiania — are my speciality. You need new pyjamas.
G.D.

Did he indeed? He hadn't noticed, but found he did. As for Parmigiania . . . He viewed such culinary sophistication with suspicion. Still, being able to entertain at home certainly had possibilities. Very definite possibilities. And quite practical advantages. For he'd been told, though not yet officially, that Campbell was to be eased from his position as Branch Supervisor (his capacity to advance beyond that to Assistant State Manager and State Manager being doubted) and that he, Naylor, was to move to that position within a month.

He was determined that, far from suffering the fate of the unfortunate, if diligent, Campbell, he would advance those next steps of the company ladder. And on the day his appointment as Branch Supervisor was announced, he invited those who at present occupied those higher rungs, together with wives, home to dinner.

Acquainted, via the note pad, with his need, the capable G.D. had prepared all. Savouries were colourful beneath cellophane, steaks marinating in burgundy, a salad prepared, a cherry shortcake, a tin of camembert opened, bottles of burgundy and hock uncorked; a note gave precise temperatures and times for cooking the steak and warming bread rolls.

It was a most successful dinner. Other dinners followed. Visiting state managers and branch supervisors came to be regally entertained at Naylor's flat; also, if less regally, those branch managers under his supervision.

Once only, and that after many months, did any discord occur between M.N. and the reliable, capable, and unseen G.D. This followed the occasion that Naylor suppressed suspicion and with what-the-hell recklessness, wrote on the note pad: Veal Parmigiania.

He had also written: hock. G.D., however, ordained white burgundy was suited to Parmigiania; and the combination could scarsely be bettered. The browned veal afloat among a spiced tomato-based sauce and topped with white and cream-coloured cheeses that swelled and bubbled hot in the baking dish, then hung down from the serving spoon in long, teased-out, threads. Never in his life had Naylor tasted anything so succulent. Nor, it seemed, had his guest. She, for it was a she, the first he had brought to dine alone with him, not only had a second, then a third, helping — but stayed the night as well.

What occurred in the night was less successful. Next morning Naylor's guest of the night left hurriedly, without breakfast, or, as it transpired, a part of her clothing. Naylor's awareness of this came from the note pad:

M.N.
Goodevening.
Your sheets, pillow slips, shirts and underclothes washed by me. The lady's petticoat you can wash yourself or not as you choose but please remove.

G.D.

The damnable woman! The utter, utter, damnable woman! If he'd wanted a moral censor no doubt there were agencies where you could hire them; but what he paid for was someone to cook to mend to clean to tidy. *That* was what she was paid for — not to have the unmitigated gall to . . . to . . . He was so enraged he threw the cutlets and salad she had prepared into the kitchen tidy, slammed the front door as he went out, then ate at a restaurant. The meal there, and the wine (which he had recently taken to drinking) soothed him to at least acknowledge, damnable gall or not, he was unlikely to find another as good.

On returning to the flat, it was this thought that caused him to take the petticoat from under the pillow where it had been left, and to walk the streets until he found someone's garbage bin where he deposited both.

Yet he lay without sleeping. For the first time he began to wonder about the unseen and unknown G.D. Was she married, he wondered. Widowed? Working to support a family? An unmarried mother? Working to keep at bay suburban boredom? Young — and working her way through university? His own age, and lonely, lying awake at that moment and hearing the dark part of her cry out her loneliness? Did she yearn to be kindled by a love affair, or long for the steady glow of friendship?

He tried by an effort of will to concentrate on how to replace Wilcocks as Assistant State Manager; but his own dark hunger gnawed at the picture of himself occupying the desk marked Assistant Manager until that picture was chewed to shreds and in the now vacant space a dark mouth was calling: G.D. . . . G.D. . . .

Abruptly he sat in the bed. Had his thoughts drifted into dream? Or had he been stark awake and was it only the well-lit and familiar part that had nodded, leaving the dark part to career unchecked down unknown and rut-crossed tracks that threatened to topple him?

Shaking his head to clear it, he decided what was needed was action. Decisive action. Decisively, then, he swung feet to floor, passed through the lounge to the note pad, wrote:

> Dear G.D.
>
> Goodmorning.

He tore out and decisively crumpled that page, wrote with even greater decision on the next:

> G.D.
>
> Your services to me have been most efficient and helpful and conducted with honesty beyond reproach. I have therefore decided upon an increment to your salary, commencing Wednesday next. I trust the amount will be to your satisfaction.
>
> M.N.

Though it was yet hours till daylight, Naylor showered, shaved, dressed, then drove through pools of light from street-lamps, to his office.

That evening, pencilled words of formal thanks appeared on the note pad which were repeated on Wednesday next. Naylor's days and even much of his nights were spent in a frenzy of work which ensured the nights were spent in a stupor of sleep.

Such work had, in time, its reward, and Wilcocks was moved out from his position of Assistant Manager, and Naylor moved in. Branch managers and their wives no longer received invitations to Naylor's flat; now it was clients of his firm to whom his secretary (for now he had a secretary) addressed invitations. For those occasions the unknown G.D. prepared and performed with full artistry, for Naylor no longer held in suspicion her abilities but gave *carte blanche* to perform what culinary arts she chose. The delights of his table became famous among clients.

His change of furniture within the company

brought to mind a change in furnishings at home was now in order. His present furnishings had been selected from a catalogue with regard to serviceability, not, as was now in his mind, to present, or (as he preferred to think) to *project*, himself among his guests of clients and company elite.

As to what colours, shapes, textures, would project him into the regard of others as he desired to be, he had not the least idea. Where could one uncover such information? And having uncovered, to discover — what shops, what warehouses, what designers and tradespeople, did one consult and employ? Above all — where did one find the time?

The solution came to him: G.D. Of course, G.D.

He left pages of notes; he signed cheques; he saw his quite ordinary flat metamorphosed into what might well have been rooms from a gentlemens' club. Wallpaper was replaced by dark panelled wood, and chairs, lounge-suite and sills upholstered in deep red leather; windows curtained in burgundy; a trio of vintage cars in ink-line and wash replaced the spirograph, and glassware was whisked away to be replaced by goblets and tankards of dull-finish stainless steel.

If his hand hesitated over some of the cheques he signed, the result was, he reflected, really an investment. A quite sound investment. And one which came to yield dividends even sooner than expected. For the state manager, pressed by the volume of work performed by his assistant and spurred by meaningful looks passed between head-office hierarchy, commenced pacing work for work with the younger man. The series of heart attacks this induced required Naylor to take over the manager's duties if not, as yet, his office, secretary, and title.

It was then some three years since Naylor had moved to the flat and engaged the unseen G.D., more than two years since the night when his own denied longings had stormed the drowsing guards of his mind to call her initials.

One evening, he found written on the notepad:

Dear M.N.

Goodevening.

From Thursday I will be going into hospital for a few days. I have arranged for a Mrs Nance Edwards to look after you during the days I'll be away and have instructed Mrs Edwards as to your needs, favourite dinners etc. I am sure you will find Mrs Edwards most satisfactory.

G.D.

As Naylor was at that time performing both the duties of State Manager as well as those of Assistant State Manager, he had little time to reflect on G.D.'s absence. There was, in fact, little to remind him as meals were left ready, flat cleaned, shirts ironed, socks and underclothes washed, folded, and put in drawers as before.

On a day when he worked late, ate in town, returned to again work before driving to his flat, he went straight to bed without a glance at the note pad. In the morning, he read:

Dear M.N.

Gwenith Dawson died yesterday in hospital. The funeral is tomorrow. If you like I will continue permanently or stay until you get someone else.

N.E.

Naylor, with the slow comprehension of having just awakened, at first wondered what on earth the death of this Gwenith Dawson had to do with him. Then he stood staring at the note pad where now all writing seemed out of focus except for the capitalized letters: G . . . D . . .

Recalling that he must leave early to meet the head office contingent at the airport, sent him racing to the shower. In the middle of shaving he stopped on the realization that the 'tomorrow' of the note was today. But he was late, late, and he left the flat without breakfast, to speed along the already crowded freeway.

Late in the morning he remembered the note, and left the head office trio long enough to tell his secretary to look up funeral notices and send flowers. What flowers would she have liked? the secretary wanted to know. Just flowers, Naylor said. But pay top price.

That night Naylor entertained with dinner at his flat, and late in the night was told he could appoint for himself an assistant. There were smiles and glasses of port all 'round at that, for all understood the implication: he was now state manager in fact, even if, for form's sake and to avoid certain unpleasantness, it might be months before he was acknowledged so in title.

The following morning was occupied in selecting an assistant, the afternoon with a lunch that continued over brandy and cigars until Naylor drove the three to the airport for the five-fifteen 'plane.

He returned to the office, but found work impossible because of the brandy. A meal, he decided, was what was needed; then back to work. But the knowledge that he had achieved state-managership was as heady as brandy and swamped his resolve, so that he celebrated over a bottle of claret with his meal, then drove, not back to work, but to the flat.

He steadied himself against the doorframe to fit key to lock. When he swung open the door he stood in the open doorway, feeling more tired than he could remember. He began to undress as he crossed to the bedroom and was down to underclothes before he lifted the pillow.

No pyjamas.

He turned to the wardrobe and pulled out the second drawer from the bottom. No neatly folded pyjamas on top. He began to rumage among socks, underpants, singlets — no, no, no pyjamas. He jerked the drawer fully out, tipping its contents on the floor and kicking among the heap of clothes. Not one pair of pyjamas! Not one! He smashed the drawer down on the tail of the bed and smashed it and smashed again until all that remained intact was the front board and the handle he held.

In the state he was in it had not occurred to him to look in another drawer or to go to bed in underclothes or the raw. On a thought he rushed to the note pad. He wrote:

G.D.

Not one pair of -

Then he remembered he was not writing to G.D. at all. G.D. had died. And as abruptly as his anger had flared, it was extinguished. He returned to the bedroom, to stand looking down at the clothes strewn everywhere, at the broken and splintered wood.

So, he thought, this is what it has come to. He had been unmoved at G.D.'s death, but driven to a frenzy of destruction over a pair of pyjamas. This was what he had made of himself. At work he pushed a button and a lift rose for him or a dictaphone accepted his words: here he wrote notes on a pad and the flat was changed or a dinner prepared or cuffs turned.

He turned to the lounge where the red leather, the dark wood and burgundy curtains seemed a part of what he had become. Towards this part his anger flared and he stalked around the flat stabbing a finger at leather, at wood, at stainless steel goblets. Abruptly he stopped as his mind shaped the questions: Could he reshape his life? Could he break from what he had made of himself?

One thing was certain: if he was to change his life, that change could not begin here in this flat. The flat was so much a part of what he had become, any change would have to begin where he had made the turning he had followed to this destination. And that point of turning had been before he moved to the flat; that point had been with Joyce.

Naylor had not seen her, beyond twice in a solicitor's office, since the day she left him. He had heard the little-known and seldom-exhibited artist had completed a maternity series of Joyce with child, which gained for him both a sell-out solo exhibition and some fame. Sufficient of both to cause him to pack brushes and depart for London, leaving Joyce and child.

If he was to remake his life, perhaps with Joyce and the baby would be where he would have to begin, even if that beginning was no more than an offer of help and friendship that had nothing calculated about it. But before he began to search out and find her, he would leave the flat.

After a night of little sleep, Naylor showered himself to wakefulness. The revelations of the night weighed on him as he stood before the note pad. Unable to decide upon the precise acts necessary to put his resolve to effect, he postponed decision and wrote instead:

N.E.
Goodmorning.
For one, Veal Parmigiana.
M.N.

Tired, tired as he was, the routines and requirements of work asserted themselves and the morning was spent in meetings with his assistant manager, his branch supervisor, his purchasing officer; the afternoon in arranging promotions, demotions, an early retirement.

Not until he returned to the flat did Naylor again reflect on his resolve of the previous night; and then only to agree with himself to postpone thought on that until after he had eaten.

It occurred to him N.E. might be unfamiliar or inept at Parmigiania, but hurrying to the 'fridge he saw the baking dish and instructions for pre-heating the oven and cooking, he saw the salad, the opened tin of camembert, the uncorked and chilled bottle of white burgundy.

He poured a glass while the oven was pre-heating, and another before he removed the dish from the oven. Removing the lid, he peered through steam at cheese swelling and bubbling among sauce and veal. The cheese hung down in long threads from the serving spoon, then from his fork. N.E. had certainly been instructed well — Naylor could not recall enjoying Parmigiania more. After he twice refilled his plate, Naylor settled back to finish the wine with some cheese. He recalled his resolve of the previous night. His resolve to do with Joyce. With Joyce and the flat. With leaving the flat.

He took the cheese, the bottle and a glass, to the divan and sat on the red leather. Pouring a glass, he looked up at wood panelling, at the red upholstered chairs and window sills, at the drapes. The effect was certainly impressive, the effect *had* impressed. He had paid a solid price; but it was a sound investment.

Emptying that glass, then refilling, he returned his attention to his resolve. What *had* prompted it in the first place? Some connection between G.D's death and pyjamas. Huh! — he smiled at that: pyjamas . . . Getting in a tizz over pyjamas. And over that he'd resolved to leave the flat!

He swung both feet onto the divan and sprawled along it. Find Joyce, leave the flat? Why should he? Everything here was so convenient and just-right, everything so very, very, satisfactory.

Dogs, in Denpasar

The dogs of the Balinese (wrote an entranced traveller of the 1930s) were undoubtedly provided by the gods to keep Bali from perfection.

Forty years later, perfection is still kept from the Balinese by their dogs. Within hotel grounds by day, dogs inhabit the gardens; by night while guests dine beneath the moon, uninvited canines slink in banana palm shadows waiting to move in for beneath-table lickings. To walk roads at night is to have one's way proclaimed in yelpings, howling and barking; to visit is to have heels snapped at. And in the villages, dogs fill the night with an oratorio composed in Hell. Black, dun, tan, yellow, patched or hyena-striped, the dogs are always (to Australian eyes) dingo-shaped.

It was Australian eyes that watched as the hotel bus unflinchingly skittled one dog, and by miracle alone missed others. Missed-by-miracle, too, were women carrying on head basket on basket on basket, cyclists, motor cyclists, beamus, jinkers jingled along by belled Timor ponies, children returning from school with banana leaves for umbrellas, men carrying fighting cocks in baskets to set down in shop-front shade; and at the city outskirts boys clothed in hat and nothing leading lethal-horned buffalos, and old men followed by their regiment of ducks; this, as the bus careered through the narrow streets, the clothe-drenching humidity, the peanut-oil and clove-scented cigarette smells, that is Denpasar at noon.

The bus took the road to the airport. There, eyes in pairs again assume bodies that are irrigated with sweat and decidedly, oh decidedly, with a thirst.

One, emerging from the bus, waves a multi-ringed hand toward the airport lounge dimness. Leaving details of luggage, of ticket, of Customs, to hotel-or-airport-employed menials, she defies the languor inducements of heat to flounce up steps and through the lounge to the bar. There she, who waved, is awaited by she, who is perched on a bar stool. The two kiss, order, bottom-up with the alacrity of stevedores. Fill-'er-ups instantly ordered, she who has waited enquires:

'Mary, Mary — how does your holiday go?'

To which is replied:

'With Balinese guides and one-night amours and free-spending roues in a row.'

Such brandy-and-dry witticisms are from (a) one who has spent eight days in Bali en-route on her yearly migration from husband in Sydney to lover in Singapore, and (b) one who for the first time is *sans* husband, *sans* kids. She, primed on suburban-told tales, has come long-way-round to join the others' last-lap dash to what night clubs, what restaurants, what drinks, what amours, a dozen Singapore nights can provide.

'I'm aching, positively aching, to tell,' she of roues-in-a-row wit says. 'That Ethridge female . . . But I told you, I positively must have. Last year . . . Same hotel . . .'

'Ohh — a Miss, wasn't she?'

'She'd missed. She certainly had.'

'Thirtyish . . .?'

'Such charity, darling, borders perjury. But memory has hit its mark. MISS Ethridge. And last year the first in her 30-plus-plus-plus years she'd tried her wings beyond the mother-dominated nest. Up she goes, flying; down she comes — in Bali. But not down-to-earth. No, ab-so-LUTELY no. She's still flying. The culture, she kept cooing. The culture! Morning — all and every morning — she spent boning up on all that Rama-and-Sita jazz; afternoons she searches for temples to drool over — temples, darling: the place is positively littered with temples and she SEARCHES for them! — then at night she goes to temple dances, shadow plays. — She even marched off one Sunday to the cockfights.'

'Uggh!'

'True, too true. But what I didn't have even the teeniest inkling of last year, was this: Her last-night-but-one was Full Moon Festival, where hotel guests and staff dance 'neath the moon all night long, and Miss Ethridge found herself dancing rumba, dancing fox-trot, dancing cheek-to-cheek, with her own Prince Rama. And love came to Miss Ethridge.'

'She didn't!'

'No quick-between-the-sheets for Miss Ethridge. Two days later she left for Melbourne and Mother. Then for six months she learnt Indonesian at night, exhausted whole libraries on Hinduism, from books tried to learn Balinese, high, low, and middle. Then to Bali she comes again. This time for three weeks. As missed as ever, she returns to Mother; but with proclamations of marriage. Her true, true love is Bali; the man who loves her with a true, true love is Balinese: ergo, marry the man and she becomes Balinese. Become Balinese and she can live her whole life through in Bali.'

'Darling, let's have another drink. But don't — please don't — stop talking.'

'Whose shout? Who cares! Because what's so positively and screamingly funny is — it was Wayang!'

Faced with laughter that is positively and screamingly funny, funny, the other hesitates before asking:

'Wayang?'

'But of course you couldn't know. Last year . . . the year before . . . Wayang was one.'

'One . . .? Ohh! — you mean: You and he . . .?'

'After an unrelieved year of Kenneth and those two

monsters I've spawned — and a week to go to Max in Singers — a Balinese bell-captain hath his charm. Oh, only early days — until something better turned up. But enough to know Wayang past, present, and what he dreams as his future. And Wayang has had the whole Rama-and-Sita-legong-cockfight-and-monkey-dance bit right up to his filed teeth. And what Wayang has his almond optics positively fixed on and zoomed up large — is the land of rolling plains. He dreams through his bell-captain days; to work, really work, at amour for lady guests at night. He's flying higher than she: he unswervingly believes that one amour will turn into the parachute he needs to brolly-hop down to where Holdens grow on gumtrees, and quadraphonic cassette players pop out of the pouches of kangaroos.'

'It's too much! She's set to marry him so she can live in Bali, while he's marrying her to live in — Oh, much too much! . . . But surely her family . . .?

'No brothers, no sisters. And Father, I gather, long since slipped off the planet.'

'Leaving Mother. And Mother . . .?'

'More drinkies?'

'Wha-a-a-t? Oh, twist my arm, darling. Twist my arm.'

Between them, silence; seldom-heard silence. Drinks are brought, bought, and with studied deliberateness carried across the now crowded lounge by one; the other, nonplussed, following.

Non-plussed asks:

'Why, oh why desert the front line?'

A multi-ringed finger indicates a woman standing decidedly with back to bar.

'You mean that six feet of ramrod woman -'

' — and ramrod morals — is Mother. Of such stuff, darling, are Methodist Ladies Guilds made.'

'I can just imagine how she took the pronouncement of marriage!'

'Then imagine this: Miss Ethridge, besotted on all things Balinese, sets about convincing Mother that if only Mother sees Bali and Wayang — all objections will evaporate in the peanut-oil-scented Balinese air. Convinced or not, Mother, as you see, has come. But that old boiler is feet-on-the-ground and no fool. It only took enough time for Wayang to drive them in a borrowed car from the airport to the hotel bungalow for Mother to read Wayang from Genesis to Revelations. And as soon as Wayang is back at his bell-captain desk, Mother took the wrappers off her whole fleet of objections, then launched new ones as well. But if Miss Ethridge couldn't see the Wayang her mother saw, she certainly knew Mother. Not a word, not a syllable, did she retaliate. Instead she took Mother to dinner (diplomatically, without Wayang), followed this with a moonlight stroll through the gardens, then guided Mother back to the bungalow door. And there, right there outside the door, she fired the torpedo which sank Mother's whole flotilla of objections in one.'

From ceiling-hung speakers commence pronouncements in one language then another and another — Singapore sounding clear in each.

'Miss Ethridge arrives,' tale-teller tells. 'On cue and crossing to Mother.'

'But, darling — surely I'm seeing double. And that dress! Red roses on white from neck to knee — do they still make dresses like that?'

'Did they EVER make dresses like that! And I'd wager drinkies for a day that beneath the roses is the olde worlde whiff of lavender water . . . But bottom-up and move, darling, what these first-timers don't know is its free drinks on board from here to Jakarta.'

Through glare suspended above the tarmac, is implored:

'The torpedo, darling. Sink me.'

'Hand on the bungalow doorhandle, Miss Ethridge

explains to Mother with the serenity of a Socrates, that the custom in Bali is for the honeymoon to precede the wedding; therefore she has arranged a second bungalow for herself and Wayang. While Mother is stumped for a syllable, Miss Ethridge opens the door, closes it after Mother goes in, proceeds to the next bungalow and to Wayang.'

'Priceless! But surely all this didn't come to you from I-spy-with-my-little-eye?'

'The hotel gardens are full of eyes and ears, the village full of mouths. And every mouth is laughing. "Wayang get kit from government clinic," the laughing mouths say. "Kit for new government program: not more than two babies each family." It's all a big joke to them. Later the joke was: "Wayang not stay with her this week — she have menstruation!" '

'Charming.'

'Think so? Then try this for charm: When her menses are over, Wayang — Wayang who dreams of Holdens, Wayang all set to bail out of Bali, Wayang brings the priest to purify her with holy water before he even steps inside the bungalow.'

'And Mother?'

'Daughter knows her mother. From full-front opposition Mother has turned about. Now she (knowing less, perhaps, than we) is not only pushing Daughter to marry — but marry as quick as she can! . . . Opposition has been as completely swallowed as a loser at the cockfights.'

First on board, first to order drinks; astonished to be told no brandy-and-dry, reduced, then, to gin-and-tonics, Teller tells:

'Having had the honeymoon, in three months Miss Ethridge is to fly back for the wedding.'

Within the other, giggles are gathering to rise. Valiantly she wages inner warfare to suppress rising giggles. Without even a solitary yelp of giggle, she manages to say:

'When her feet finally touch ground — how will she live in Bali?'

To which is replied:

'If Wayang achieves what his sights are fixed on — how will he live in Australia?'

Giggles that are loaded with brandy-and-dry, primed on gin-and-tonic, cannot avoid their launching. Explosively, the giggles launch themselves to yelp and howl in uncontrollable, bent-to-knees, laughter. Ignited by laughter that propels her companion forward, the other's laughter propels her back against the aisle seat to laugh with open throat where through streaming eyes she sees the two unusually tall women, distortedly glimpses roses on white, inhales what instantly she identifies as — yes! — lavender water.

The plane door is snapped closed, shutting out the smells of peanut-oil and clove-scented cigarettes, the smell of Bali.

Airborne and with the now expired laughter replaced by languor, she who was touched by the roses, says:

'Singers-here-we-come!'

Then, closing eyes and smiling: 'I hope Max is waiting.'

The other, eyes already closed, says:

'I hope he's brought a friend.'

And on the ground dogs languid in noontide shade, close their lids. Later they will open them to slink in for beneath-table lickings, to chorus their oratorio from Hell, to snap at heels, to yelp and howl at others journeying in the dark: Performing that task appointed them by the gods — to keep the Balinese, keep us all, from perfection.

The Picking Season

Beyond a window of the single-carriage train, twin concrete cylinders of a wheat silo loomed above low Mallee scrub; and another of the pickers said, 'This's it.'

When I wheeled my bike along the platform, pickers with their suitcases clustered around a spike-topped gate. Beyond the gate dried leathery faces examined us from beneath turned-down brims.

'I'll take the kid with a bike.'

Awkwardly, I wheeled the bike forward; then a hand closed around mine holding the suitcase and took it from me.

I followed to a dented utility truck, caked in red mud; and hefted the bike in on top of the case.

'Name's Ron,' he said. 'Ron Quin. Hop in.'

We drove from the railway station and the silos, the car splashing through puddles in potholes. Late afternoon sun drew steam from rain-darkened bitumen. Past shops hooded by verandahs and a pub, the low Mallee scrub began.

'Bloody rain,' he said. 'F' eight months o' the year, y'd go down on yer knees f' rain . . . But once the fruit's on the vines, y'd rather sight a debt-collector than rain — and down she comes! . . . with rain in this heat the fruit rots while yer watchin' it.'

The bitumen ended. A red sandy track went on, through spindly stunted scrub.

'Specially with the pickers I won,' he said, continuing, after a distance of miles, his previous statement. 'One had the shakes from booze. Walked off. The two I still got are German. They don't like the heat, they don't like the dust, they won't get down on their knees . . . I'll tell y' something right now: you stand-'n'-bend — like them Germans — you won't make wages. An' I won't get enough o' the crop off t' *pay* wages!'

He was in his thirties. Short and sinewy, his limbs emerging from dirty shorts and stain-streaked shirt were the colour of the red sandy track darkened by rain.

The track emerged from the stunted scrub. Rows of vines along waist-high wires filled an uncannily flat landscape. Among the green were pickers and tractors pulling trailers loaded with rectangular iron buckets.

Ron turned in at a gateway, drove around behind a fibro-cement house, past drying racks, to stop in front of a corrugated iron hut.

'Two spare bunks in there. Take either one.'

My new employer stepped straight from the ute's cabin, onto the seat of a tractor.

Inside the hut, bunks had been made by threading sapling trunks through hessian bags. Nails driven into the unlined frame provided means of hanging clothes. Empty fruit-boxes served as cupboards.

I was arranging clothes, tinned food, books, when the sound of voices drew me to the door.

The lowering sun tinged the vines in mauve light. There was a stillness in which distant sounds of tractors seemed to hang in the mauve air.

Two figures came slowly between the rows of vines. One was short and heavy. He wore only shorts, boots, hat; his body was burned brown by the sun. The other was taller, lighter built. He wore long trousers, his shirt sleeves were buttoned at the wrist, his collar turned up about his neck.

Closer, the short heavy one called out his name to me.

'Helmut.'

Immediately he began saying he'd been in Australia before. He'd worked two years on the Transcontinental Railway.

'But him,' he indicated the tall one. 'I tell on the boat: I will learn you English. But he all-a-time at night in the cabin with lady. Daytime he so weak he on hands an' foots like a dog.'

Helmut dropped to all fours, head hanging down, tongue out, panting. Then he lifted his head to emit dog-on-heat yelps and howls.

I'd begun to laugh at Helmut's clowning, when the other shouted something at him. No need to comprehend the language to apprehend the meaning: if Helmut thought of this shipboard romance as a dog-on-heat affair, the other did not.

The tall German took out his anger in kicking his bootsoles against a plowshare set upright for the purpose of scraping mud from boots. Not until Helmut had gone to the side of the hut where a shower had been rigged beneath a tankstand, did the other address me.

'Helmut . . . er . . . Helmut *grose* Charlie Chaplin.'

He indicated himself.

'Alf.'

Outside the hut, he took off his boots. Inside, he took off his trousers. With morose humour he demonstrated the trousers would stand — almost — unsupported. He took off his shirt.

Alf must have begun picking in just shorts, for his back was covered in watery blisters of sunburn. Down the backs of his legs, skin was peeling away. When he turned toward me, I saw his thighs covered in blisters that had burst, then an irritation — perhaps from the grape juice or the red dust — had set up infection. At the back and sides of his neck were blisters margined by inflammation.

In the open fireplace of the hut, he got a fire going. He heated water to bathe his blisters. Later, Helmut returned from the house where their meat was kept in the fridge. Throughout their meal, Alf barely spoke. When Helmut took out a pack of cards, Alf pointedly took out a book.

I joined Helmut in playing cards for matches, and in spite of the fire began to feel the cold. I went to my case for a jumper. Then Alf, sitting on his bunk with blankets pulled around his shoulders, rummaged his small stock of English to say to me:

'Daytime — Sahara: nightime — Siberia.'

He threw off his blankets, stoked the fire, went out from the hut.

Helmut was telling me that in Germany after the war he had been a trotting driver. In a confusion of assertions he told of races he'd been rigged out of winning, of being robbed in photo-finishes, of the crookedness of trainers, bookmakers, drivers, judges. To escape, I stood, slapped the front of my pants, said I had to go outside.

As I closed the door, cold engulfed me with such intensity it was minutes before I could breathe freely. Hugging arms to chest, I walked to the gateway, ran along the road. But running caused the cold to burn in my throat with the taste of nausea. Beneath stars flaring with icy brilliance, I walked back the way I had run.

I had reached the gate, when I saw someone standing among the vines. The figure was quite motionless and standing just beyond a finger of light that reached out from the one illuminated window of the house.

In the cold of morning, Ron took me out among the vines. He demonstrated how to move the rectangular iron bucket along between my knees while one hand lifted the bunches and the other cut the stem and chopped away grapes that were rotting.

By the time the sun was belting down from half

way up the sky, dried juice from rotting grapes had stiffened my shirt front and thighs of my pants. But, kneeling, I was making faster progress on my row than the two Germans were on theirs. They stood and stooped and moved their buckets by hand.

Our midday meal was taken at the house. We washed face and hands, scraped boots, went in at the flywire door.

Ron introduced me to his wife: 'This's Wendy.'

There was nothing dainty or pretty about Ron's wife; though she did possess a kind of big-boned handsomeness. As she moved from stove to table, table to sink, she leaned back from the waist to ballast her pregnancy.

When we finished our cold meat, salad and bread, she said:

'You lot get yer bums down an' feet up b'fore yer out again in that bugger o' a sun.'

It was as she was pouring hot water from a kettle into the sink in front of the kitchen's solitary window, that it came to me — *this* was the illuminated window of the previous night.

Twice, that afternoon, it rained. We all ran to unroll covers down the sides of drying racks and to cover fruit drying on tarred paper on the ground. When the rain passed, the steamy heat was made even more oppressive by the stench of grapes fermenting.

That night, the three of us had washed and eaten, when Ron pushed open the door. He stood there in juice-stained shirt and shorts and hands black with grease from working on the tractor. He asked if we would work through the weekend.

I affected disinterest to see if he would offer a higher rate.

Helmut translated to Alf, who emphatically shook his head. Helmut said he wouldn't either.

Ron turned to the door. I said I'd pick. Even at the going rate I'd be making better money than I'd been making and it wasn't going to last. Not with the rain.

At this, Ron apparently decided he'd try an appeal.

'The blockie who had this before me loaded his wife 'n' kids 'n' kitchen table onto his truck — an' he lit out . . . The bank got back the truck — repossessed. They never got him. I got this block with a loan the size o' that blockie's debts. First picking season I did all right. Next two — lousy. This one looked like a bumper — till the rain. Now it's a race against rot t' get enough fruit off t' keep the bank from selling me up . . . So-o-o-o, what about it?'

Alf must have understood most of that because he kept indicating his neck and back and thighs. Helmut sat shaking his head — until he was struck with an idea.

He put to Ron they would work Saturday morning if Ron would drive them the eight miles to the pub in the afternoon. They would not work Sunday.

There was little Ron could do except agree.

As it happened, neither on the Saturday nor the Sunday did it rain. Past lunch on Monday, dark slate-coloured clouds began to muster; and Ron was punching on the ute's horn to bring us running.

Throughout that week, there was sporadic rain. And twice, Alf went at night to stand motionless among the vines, staring in at the kitchen window.

When Ron asked if we'd work the weekend, Helmut put the same proposition as the week before.

On the Sunday, the two Germans slept through the morning. In the afternoon they sat in the shade of almond trees, dozing and drinking beer.

From the west, clouds blew in with such suddenness that drops were falling before we reached the racks. Neither Helmut nor Alf moved to help. Then the flywire door slammed, and Wendy came running in bare feet.

That brought Alf to his feet and running. In driving rain, he shouted at Wendy, pointing toward the house. She jerked a thumb at him, began dragging a tarpaulin to cover drying fruit. Then she ran for spare sheets of tarred paper. Alf abandoned his remonstrations, to drag tarpaulins and tarred paper and cover drying fruit beside her.

By the time Ron and I unrolled covers on the drying racks, Wendy and Alf had covered the fruit spread on tarred paper. Splashing through puddles, we all ran to the east side of the hut. Wendy made no attempt to stand against the wall. Red mud splashed up her legs, her dress clinging to her, outlining her pregnancy, she seemed to take a perverse pleasure from standing in the driving rain.

'That,' she said, 'has buggered it. There's as much chance o' me being Queen of England as there is of us keeping this place!'

Helmut had been first against the hut wall. He laughed hugely at Wendy's assertion.

Alf wanted to know what was the joke. He seemed not to comprehend either in English or in translation. Then Helmut went into a clowning act of Wendy as Queen, of subjects bowing before her.

When Alf did comprehend Wendy's meaning, it appalled him.

'Home,' he said, directly at Ron. He swept an arm around to include Wendy, the house, the fruit block.

'Home — finished?'

In his tight-lipped way, Ron said there was a chance yet.

'Huh!' Wendy said. 'Some chance!'

Helmut must have decided he had some squaring off to do for not helping; because after Ron and I had finished work, he offered to share what was left of the beer.

So when Ron had washed and eaten, he came to the hut. I wanted to get Ron talking about the war in New Guinea; but whenever we got on to that subject — or any other, it was lapped at bolting pace by Helmut's trotting horses. Helmut had a photograph of horses distorted by the angle and he was claiming it proved he had won but the judges had -

'Uhh!' Alf swept Helmut's photograph from the fruit-box. 'All-time horses trotting! — Trotting horses!'

Where Helmut's photograph had been, Alf slapped down one of his own. That creased and curled print showed a family posed in front of a two-storey house. The father and youth of, perhaps, twelve, wore hats with narrow brims and feathers in the band, white shirts beneath bib-and-leather shorts.

Ron asked if those were really the clothes they normally wore. With sullen help from Helmut, Alf said those were normal clothes in some country districts and in parts of Bavaria. Not in northern Germany where he'd lived. But in Hitler's time everyone was encouraged to dress like that on Sundays and when there were political rallies. That photograph had been taken during the first year of the war.

It was the girl in the photograph who took my interest. She was eight or nine — a year or two older than my own sister. And like my sister, she was very fair and had small-boned facial features. Mother and daughter both wore scoop-neck blouses with puff sleeves beneath a small garment laced from waist to chest, and a wide patterned skirt: an outfit Helmut told us was called a dirndle.

Alf told how he had started to learn English at school.

'I . . . go . . . to . . . the . . . window
I . . . go . . . to . . . the . . . door
I . . . come . . . from . . . the . . . window
I . . . come . . . from . . . the . . . door.'

The lessons had been stopped, he couldn't remember why.

What he did remember were Sunday mornings. He and his sister would wait in their room until they heard their father go from the other bedroom to the kitchen. Then they ran to jump into the big bed, beneath the doona with their mother. When their father brought coffee for their mother, he always expressed surprise at finding them in the bed. Alf would ask for coffee for his sister and himself because it was Sunday, and their father would sternly lecture them that coffee was not for growing children — then go to the kitchen for the two cups already poured for them.

Helmut, in filling in where Alf's English failed him, added to the telling by saying that Hannover, where Alf lived, was a big city — more people than Perth or Adelaide.

There had been little damage to the city when Alf, at sixteen, had been trucked south. That was where he met Helmut. They were both in the same anti-aircraft crew.

It was some four months after the war ended before Alf was able to make his way north. There he found that part of his home city where he had lived, a waste of fire-blackened rubble. At night he huddled with a hundred others in the shell of a church. His days were spent walking, asking, asking. None was able to tell him what he asked. He was not even able to identify individual streets.

When he left it was without even the certainty he had found where his home had been.

Throughout the dozen years since, he had moved from city to city without settling or forming any lasting relationship; until a chance meeting with Helmut, back from two years in Australia.

The following week, Helmut gained a second topic of

conversation. Ron returned from the local store with two letters. One was a letter from my mum with a postscript from my sister. The other, for Alf.

In his elation at receiving the letter, Alf told Helmut. Helmut, of course, told us. It was from the lady of Alf's shipboard romance. She was working as a nursing aide in Melbourne, and would move out from the migrant hostel as soon as she could find a flat near the hospital.

Helmut clowned his dog-on-heat act during morning and afternoon smokos. After he once got a laugh from Wendy by saying Alf would soon be working hard in the night, he said the same thing every lunch time.

Alf took this with more forebearance than he'd previously shown. But Helmut was getting on all our nerves. One lunch time, Ron told Helmut he'd better give it a rest. The next day Helmut said the same thing again. This time, Wendy bellowed at him: 'Put a bloody sock in it!'

The rest that gained us lasted more than a week. During that time, there were days without rain, and days of sudden, brief showers.

Alf's back and legs healed; though he had only to work a day without the bandage for more blisters to appear on top of infections around his neck. He never seemed to adjust to the heat, or to the fall in temperature at night. Nor to the red mud when it rained, the red dust when it didn't, the stain and stench of rotting grapes.

After Alf received the letter, a week passed before he went from the hut at night. It was a night of full moon, and I too left the hut. I stooped among vines to arrive at a point behind Alf. Framed in the kitchen window beyond Alf was Wendy at the sink and Ron supporting his head with one hand over the kitchen table. Wendy must have finished washing dishes, for she went from the sink. When she again appeared she threw a tea-towel at Ron. He made no move to catch it and the towel landed on his head. Then Wendy was again gone from the window, Ron took the towel and moved to the sink to dry dishes. They must have had a wireless playing, because when Wendy again appeared she did some dance steps around Ron, tapping him on the head as though to music. At all events, that tight-lipped man looked at her and grinned.

That was about all. Ron returned to the table; Wendy went from the window, though she must have remained in the room for at times Ron looked up and spoke.

Alf made his way back to the hut. I stooped among vines to the road, to walk miles through a flat moon-washed landscape.

When Alf's second letter arrived, he said nothing to Helmut. The following afternoon he came to where Ron and I were unrolling covers on the racks. In words he had apparently rehearsed, he said:

'Saturday . . . I go to back to Melbourne.'

Ron went on unrolling the covers as though nothing had been said. Then he went from the racks, up steps and in at the flywire door. He let the door slam after him.

Next morning, Alf was waiting for Ron beside the tractor. Word for word he said the same thing again. This time he added on the Tuesday he would 'come to back to here.'

Ron stepped up onto the tractor, cranked at the motor, drove off.

But when Ron brought black tea in a thermos for afternoon smoko, he thrust toward Alf a slip of paper with figures on it.

'That's the buckets you an' Helmut 've picked. I'll make out your cheque for half.'

Alf said he'd take his cheque with him.

'S'pose you expect me to endorse yer rail voucher too?'

That needed translating. Then Alf nodded that was what he wanted.

At night, Ron brought the cheque and the signed rail voucher to the hut. As Alf hadn't worked the full season, Ron wasn't required to sign the voucher. Now that he had, Alf would travel to Melbourne free; but if he was coming back he was up for the fare both ways.

Some chance! I thought.

Alf began to say he'd come back on the Tuesday — when Ron cut him short.

'So y'keep tellun me!'

Ron did, however, tell Alf about the trains; and it was actually Friday night that he drove Alf to the station.

Ron and I worked the Saturday and Sunday with Helmut wandering over to talk. When a shower blew up, Helmut helped us cover the drying fruit. While we waited for the rain to pass, Helmut went through his dog-on-heat antics.

And when, lunch time Tuesday, Helmut recited his piece about Alf working hard in the night, even Helmut could interpret the look he got from Ron.

That afternoon I heard the tractor motor die away, the ute start up, drive out along the road.

I was on my bunk, trying to summon enough energy to wash and cook dinner, when I heard the ute return.

Only one door slammed. And that, hard.

Next afternoon Ron drove off again. It wasn't the train he was headed for — it was the employment office. There he was told there was no hope of him getting pickers, not this late in the season.

Both the Thursday and Friday were very still, with oppressive humidity which by the Friday afternoon had turned into threat of a storm.

I walked ahead of Helmut between the rows of vines to the hut. And there he was — Alf.

Helmut came in and began immediately to blurt out questions in German, translating the answers to me. Yes, Alf had come in on today's train. He hadn't got a lift. He'd walked. Yes, walked. Carrying his case and coat he's walked the eight miles in the heat.

Alf looked done in. He lay sprawled on his bunk, staring up at the corrugated iron roof.

I went among the vines to tell Ron. He hesitated in his loading buckets of grapes onto the trailer. That hesitation was the sole indication that he'd heard.

That night the hut door was pushed open and Ron stood there holding two bottles of beer. Wendy was behind him. She had more bottles, glasses, the battery wireless from the house.

Neither said anything about Alf coming back. Ron held out his hand to Helmut for an opener, and got the tops off bottles.

Alf sat up on his bunk. Helmut, responding as always to an audience, got maximum effect by clowning as he asked questions in German, then leeringly translating to us.

Yes, Alf had stayed in the lady's flat. Yes — it had been just like on the boat. Yes — she'd planned on him staying and had even arranged a job for him at the hospital.

Then Alf spoke directly to Ron and Wendy. In his limited English, he said she (his lady friend) did not want marriage, children, home and like that. She just wanted him to live with her.

Helmut couldn't see any problem about that. He went down on hands and knees, lifting his head high to yeowl and howl.

Alf stood and he kicked Helmut. The kick thudded into Helmut's stomach and would have put most men in hospital. It didn't do that to Helmut. He got to his feet with one hand holding his stomach the other clenched into a fist and he came at Alf.

Ron stepped in front of Helmut, thrust a glass of beer into his hand. Wendy flung an arm around Helmut's neck and laughed. Helmut stopped his rush. He stood, puzzled. Then he must have decided the laugh was on Alf, for he skolled the beer. He roared laughing.

Wendy kept the momentum of that going by switching on the wireless. She turned through stations and static until she had music. She held out her arms to Helmut to dance with her.

To a strident beat they danced something between a jive and a jitterbug. Wendy tossed off a glass of beer as she danced, without missing a beat. And Helmut stuck out his belly as he danced in clowning imitation of Wendy's pregnancy.

The music ended with Wendy laughing, breathless and perspiring. Ron filled glasses, while Wendy fiddled with the wireless. The music she next found was more sedate. Alf came to Ron to quite formally ask if he could dance with Wendy.

The dance of Wendy and Alf didn't work very well. Alf tried to dance something like a waltz, then more like a foxtrot. They couldn't get the steps right. And Alf became embarrassed because of Wendy's protruding belly against him. Then Wendy became embarrassed because he was. They both seemed relieved when the music ended.

Alf led Wendy to Ron; then went to his case. The parcel he took from it and gave to Wendy was, he said, for the baby. What Wendy opened was a tiny blouse, jacket, skirt: miniatures of what Alf's mother and sister wore in the photograph.

The present struck me as ridiculous. The baby might not be a girl! Even if it was, a dirndle — here — would be as misplaced as a didgeridoo in a military brass band!

Wendy seemed mystified by the present, too. Oh, she thanked him — kissed him full on the lips — and Ron clapped his shoulder in thanks. But plainly Wendy did not know what she would ever do with it.

Holding the dirndle in front of her, she jived to a pulsating beat from the wireless.

We'd all had a couple of glasses by then; and us three pickers stood around her, clapping and shouting, as she — incredibly for her size and state — went to it. She stomped, rocked hips, shoulders, shook arms and breasts, her hair flying out, her head tossed back in laughter. Ron did not stand and clap. He sat grinning at Wendy's dance and at our applause: in his own way taking more from it than any of us.

Past Wendy, I saw the grin go from Ron. He reached for the wireless — switched off. Then we all heard it. Rain. Rain not yet on the iron roof; but advancing, tramping across the rows of vines. Then it was upon us, larruping on the iron roof and the walls, holding us silent within its kettledrum rattattoo.

Fritz

A straggling line of troops tramp across wooden slats joined into duckboards that zig-zag across a sea of mud. The duckboards-on-mud stretch further than the troops can see. They lead to a line of trenches these same Australians occupied almost a year before.

When last he walked these duckboards, Private Oberdiah Hobbs walked in the knowledge he had been one among those who stormed the hot and stony hills of Gallipoli and had fought as heroes. Neither the last days there spent clearing and planting wattle around the graves of those who would not be returning, nor in knowing the campaign had been bungled to failure, had taken from him that knowledge.

The previous time, the town through which they passed was whole and inhabited. The church did not, then, gape open-roofed to the sky. There was not the howitzer they now passed, bogged above its axles in mud.

That time, some were singing the song of the town.

Mademoiselle from Armentieres

Parley voo

Hasn't been humped for fifty years

Parley voo.

Others were chiacking the singers with comments as ribald as the song.

This time, the troops tramp silently. Oberdiah wears the helmet of one who sang, he carries the rifle of one who chiacked — two destroyed, among more than half the company's number, in battles that raged in the valley of the River Somme.

There — after the big guns had roared all night — Oberdiah had been among those who crossed No-Man's-Land in the before-dawn dark. By daylight they occupied the first line of enemy trenches. Past noon enemy guns began shelling what had previously been their own trenchline. Abruptly the shelling stopped. Oberdiah saw troops with fixed bayonets and stick bombs streaming towards him across open ground and along interconnecting trenches.

By nightfall he was one of many fleeing and being shot down across the same ground over which they had advanced.

The night veiled from Oberdiah, veiled from men of both armies, what the morning sun revealed to be a scene of horror.

Right across No-Man's-Land men lay groaning or calling out and raising an arm.

Soon stretcher-bearers from each side were out working under Red Cross flags. But the stretcher-bearers so few, the wounded so many.

Some Australians tied a rag to a pick-handle and climbed over the parapet of sandbags, out into No-Man's-Land. Then German soldiers could be seen working under improvised flags with their own stretcher-bearers.

An Allied observation plane flew low over No-Man's-Land, followed by a runner to the front trenches. An officer read aloud the order.

'There must be no collaboration of any kind with the enemy. Immunity from being fired upon currently being granted enemy troops under improvised flags — must cease. Except in the case of bona-fide stretcher-bearers under a flag exactly as prescribed in the Rules Of War — all observed enemy troops must be fired on.'

The officer moved along the trench reading the stiff and formal phrasing of the order. He did not comment on what he read, but after reading to one group of men he moved on to the next.

All along the parapet of sandbags troops looked out across No-Man's-Land where now the sun beat down, bringing flies and ants to further torment the wounded.

A staring face next to Oberdiah's own, addressed him.

'Y' wouldn't take odds at 'undred-t'-one with bad money on the chances of some of 'em. Not now, eh?'

Oberdiah did not answer. He turned from the face that had addressed him, to another.

'One thing's f' sure,' this other said. 'That's put paid to a lot of 'em making it past the finishing post.'

Within Oberdiah the certainty was proclaiming itself that the one chance most of the wounded had of living, lay in troops not obeying that order.

But how to proclaim such a certainty to others?

During days of drill and parade, obedience to orders had been instilled as the sole morality of war. When they were in the valley of the Somme, these Australians had seen French and British troops whose own terror or judgement had brought them to disobey orders, crumple before firing squads. There were stories of executions by the enemy of his own.

The troops grumbled and complained — yet bolstered each other to accept what they complained of.

'Obey and grumble,' they told each other. 'But obey.'

What possibility, then, of Oberdiah proclaiming his certainty along the trenchline?

It transpired that the object of his certainty came to be gained without him doing anything, much less anything heroic. For the officer, who was a field officer and reckoned by the troops to be a good one, did not give the expected orders that would put into effect the order sent by runner from the behind-lines brass. Having read aloud the order along that section of the front, he left the trenches.

None of the Australians fired on enemy troops working under improvised flags with the stretcher-bearers, and none of their own were fired on.

This brought Oberdiah the comfort of thinking to speak his certainty not only had not been necessary — but would not during future events be so.

That comfort was soon to be taken from him.

A night raid on enemy trenches resulted in prisoners being brought in. Oberdiah stood guard, as prisoners were taken in twos and threes along the interconnecting trenches. One prisoner lay on the floor of the trench. He had one bloodstained leg of his trousers cut away and blood seeped through his field dressing.

For some reason there was delay in getting stretcher-bearers to the trench. After other prisoners had been taken along interconnecting trenches, Oberdiah gave the wounded prisoner a cigarette.

'Thank you.'

Though surprised at being addressed in English, Oberdiah was not drawn into conversation. The prisoner drew gratefully on the cigarette. Then in accented words he enquired if Oberdiah had been here when soldiers had worked with stretcher-bearers in bringing in the wounded.

Oberdiah did not reply. Giving a wounded prisoner a cigarette was one thing — fraternizing with him quite another.

Perhaps it was because for him the war was over, but the prisoner had no such inhibition.

'Ve did goot, *ja*?'

He smoked for a moment, then answered his own question.

'*Ja*, ve did goot.'

Then he told of an officer coming to their trench-line, of a similar order being read aloud in the German trenches. This officer did not go from one group of men to the next. He commanded the order be shouted from man to man along that section of the front.

'Ve shouted — all enemies must be shot at. *Ja* — all along d' line ve shout dat. All troops stand up on d' firing step. Then other words vos passed man to man. Not a shout, dis time. No. A visper. Dat visper vent all along d' line. Ve stood on d' firing step — but obeyed d' visper . . . Ve did goot, *ja*? If they don't fire on ours, ve vispered, ve don't fire on theirs.'

Soon stretcher-bearers came and the wounded prisoner was taken. His story stayed. Oberdiah constantly thought of that whisper being passed from man to man along the firing step. No doubt it was passed furtively at first; then, as it came to be accepted, with the implication of threat to any who did not obey it. He imagined the soldier who might first have whispered it — sweating, his mouth parched dry with fear of the consequences if his whisper was not accepted and he was renounced.

That soldier, it seemed to Oberdiah, had achieved a victory of a kind. An austere and very personal victory. But one which no future retreat or defeat could take from him.

So when Oberdiah Hobbs tramped duckboards toward the trenches outside of Armentieres, he no longer held any belief that the duckboards across mud were a path to glory.

He soon found the fighting to be at such a stalemate that the Allied order specified a maximum of a hundred and fifty men plus one big gun to each thousand yard sector.

Soldiers of each side looked out from their parapet of sandbags across three hundred yards of barbed wire and shell craters and mud, to the enemy parapets. Few raids were attempted. Each side sporadically shelled the other and sniped from firing slots in the parapets.

If the fighting was light compared with what they

had been through, the Australians soon discovered in addition to the enemy in front — who they called Fritz — and those they regarded as the enemy behind — who they called The Brass — there now came an enemy more merciless than either. That enemy was winter.

Drifts of freezing rain shrouded the whole battlefield. Water rose in the trenches, first over the duckboards then into dugouts where men huddled to sleep.

Months passed in rain, while each trenchline shelled and sniped at the other. In the Australians' sector were few interconnecting trenches and no stretcher-bearers. Those who became wounded had to lie all day in wet dugouts until they could be taken out on a soldier's back at night.

To torments that differed only in detail from those endured by the rest of the front, the trenches out from Armentieres proved to have two peculiarly their own.

The bread ration stood at one loaf between eight men every two days. There was no tea. Nothing cooked or hot. To each sector was assigned a mobile cookhouse; but its smokestack and smoke would provide the enemy such a perfect target, it was left somewhere back from the front and never used. Strangely, there was plenty of jam and plenty of cheese. Men spread jam on cheese and that's mostly what they lived on, right through that winter.

Then there were *coodies*. Smaller than fleas, *coodies* hived in the seams of clothes and blankets. No matter how the *coodies* bit while men were standing and moving, their full assault came when men attempted to sleep. Soldiers threw off blankets to tear at clothes and to scratch and scratch until there was blood under their nails. On the rare days free of rain, soldiers in turn crouched naked and shivering over a candle flame through which they passed seams of blankets and clothes. A stench as when a blacksmith burns the iron shoe onto a horse's hoof, puffed up as each nest of *coodies* was caught in the flame.

Christmas brought neither warmth nor cheer, and the New Year added first fog, then frost. The floor of the trenches set solid in ice. In the dugouts stalactites of ice forced men to wear battle helmets even during their attempts to sleep.

That frost lay on the ground for seven weeks.

One morning, the fog suddenly lifted. Sunlight flared on frozen puddles across No-Man's-Land and shot glints of light from icicles beneath barbed wire.

Oberdiah came from his dugout to hold his hands up to the brightness. All along the trench men stood in the thin sun-warmth.

'Hey! — there's a Fritz waving at us!'

A sentry's shout sent men jostling each other to peer through firing slots. Oberdiah at first saw only the line of enemy parapets. Then an arm appeared above the sandbags, waved quickly, was gone. The arm appeared again, waved, retracted. From another point of the enemy sandbags — another wave. Then another.

Some wag among the Australians waved in return. No shots came. Soon they were all at it, arms waving to answering waves from the far side of No-Man's-Land.

No one, however, showed his head above the parapet. By the time the sun was straight up in the sky, the waving had stopped.

'Fritz — he's up t' somethin'!'

At this shout from a sentry, Oberdiah rushed to a slot to see a dark shape moving and spreading along the enemy trenchline. Soon that dark . . . something . . . was right along that sector of the enemy trenches.

'Fritz's hanging out his washing!'

'Bonkers! — he's gunna come over the top right at us!'

'So's my fat aunt!'

'It's a smoke screen so we don't get a gander what he's up to!'

'Camouflage! Fritz's camouflaging his position!'

'Bulsh! — why'd he camouflage his position when we know where he is?'

Jostled from his firing slot, Oberdiah went from the arguing voices. He returned from his dugout to rest a fieldglass across the top sandbag of the parapet.

Some of those around the firing slots stopped jostling and arguing to stand around Oberdiah.

'It's blankets,' Oberdiah told them. 'Blankets — and greatcoats. Fritz's throwing his blankets and his greatcoats out over the wire. He's hanging them in the sunshine!'

Men ran to their dugouts. They returned to the parapets with blankets, greatcoats, any clothes not being worn, to throw them out over their own barbed wire.

While they were doing this — another shout from a sentry.

'There's a Fritz standing! He's standing above their parapet!'

Men snatched up rifles, rushed to the firing step, pushed barrels through slots. Yet the strangeness of anyone showing himself like that held them from firing.

Oberdiah saw him, framed in the V of his rifle sights — a figure with arms spread wide forming a cross against the clear bright sky.

All along the sector men were staring over their rifle sights at the distant, still, figure.

'What's he up to?'

'Wait t' find out — don't shoot yet!'

'Don't shoot — what's that bonkers Fritz doing?'

'Got rabies that's what!'

'Don't shoot!'

'Hey — he's moving!'

'Reckons he can come over here an' drop in f' Sunday dinner!'

Men arguing over their rifle sights saw the figure step from the sandbags, between and over wire, toward them. Keeping his arms out wide, he stepped around shell craters, slipping on ice, stopping, once falling. He kept coming on until he reached a mound and mounted it. Then he stood there, at the centre of No-Man's-Land; a human cross stark against the sky.

Even without fieldglasses, Oberdiah could see plainly the grimy boots and putties, the pockets low on the button-up-to-the-neck collarless tunic, the downturned moustache and dark stubble on a face enclosed by a balaclava and crowned — not by a spiked *pickelhaube* helmet as used during attack and bombardment — but a peakless cloth cap.

The soldier began slowly bringing his hands in toward his body. Those watching over rifle sights, saw the hands hesitate at the chest then move slowly downwards. Each hand lifted a pocket flap, slid into a pocket. The time he took to bring his hands from his pocket seemed interminable. When he did, he brought his hand up to his face and cupped them there.

He reached out to again form a cross, and the watchers saw the cigarette and the thin wisp of smoke. They saw the face turn up to the sun, as though the mind that directed it waited for something to happen.

Oberdiah never saw which Australian was first up, over, and out from the sandbags. But soon he was too. Soon they all were — holding apart and stepping through wire — barbs catching clothes — tearing free — running — falling on ice — slipping — stumbling toward the centre of No-Man's-Land.

And from the distant trenches men were running, stumbling, falling on ice, sliding and falling in their rush toward them.

Oberdiah found himself closing with a soldier he recognized as being as gaunt and grimy as himself.

'Der sonne ist schon — Ja? Ist sehr sehr schon, ja? Ja!'

Something about the sun, Oberdiah realized. The sun or the sunshine or sunwarmth.

'It's beaut, ain't it?' he said. 'Real beaut.'

Only then did it occur to him there was something lunatic about standing in the centre of No-Man's-Land discussing the weather with the enemy. The same thought must have occurred to the German, for abruptly he began to laugh. Oberdiah began to laugh too. Laugh and shake hands.

The German's laugh abruptly went from him.

'Der Krieg ist schrecklick, ja? Die essen ist schreklick. Dieser Leben ist schrecklick, dieser Tod ist schrecklick.'

Whatever the repeated word *schrecklick* meant, it was plainly something the German considered to be awful to the point of appalling. There was a great deal that appalled Oberdiah.

'This war,' he said, 'is a proper bastard.'

He saw that right across No-Man's-Land soldiers from each side were shaking hands, laughing, attempting to talk. Those of the enemy who spoke English had a crowd of Australians around them, all shouting questions. Any Australian who spoke even a few words of German was surrounded by Germans, all asking questions and repeating the answers to each other.

Oberdiah realized he was still holding the other's hand. At that, they both laughed. Disengaging hands, Oberdiah dived that hand into a tunic pocket. When he offered a cigarette — a cigarette was being offered to him. Exchanging cigarettes, they each lit the other's. The German inhaled, puffed out a stream of smoke into the chill bright air.

'Ist schon.!' Evidently he was referring to the cigarette. *'Ist schon, ja, sehr sehr schon.'*

'This's beaut,' Oberdiah held out the cigarette he had been given. 'Real beaut.'

At that moment he chanced to see the soldier who had begun it all. That soldier stood alone on his mound, gazing at those milling below him. His face had the slow sad smile of a man who'd bet all he had on a long-odds outsider, then seen it come romping home.

'Attention! Attention all Allied troops!'

A megaphone shout from the Allied trenchline.

'Attention — all Allied troops at present in No-Man's-Land. All must return to their trenches — forthwith! Repeat — all Allied troops must forthwith return to their trenches!'

Oberdiah turned to his own trenchline — and jerked his thumb. All across No-Man's-Land Australian troops jerked a thumb toward their own trenchline and at observation blimps anchored in the sky back of the trenches.

The German had taken from his tunic pocket a photograph. Before he had shown it — a megaphone shouted orders from the German trenchline. *'Actung! Actung! Alles Deutsche Soldaton! Zuruck Augenblicklick zuruck! Augenblicklick zuruck!'*

Some Germans began imitating the Australian troops in jerking their thumbs toward their own trenchline and observation blimps. Evidently the gesture was an unfamiliar one to the Germans, for they would jerk their thumbs then look to the Australian for confirmation they had performed it correctly. They laughed like children as their backs were slapped to confirm they had got it right.

'Attention! Attention! Allied troops not returning forthwith to their trenches will be fired on. Repeat — all troops in No-Man's-Land will be fired on!'

This provoked more thumb-jerking. The German with Oberdiah had an arm around Oberdiah's shoulder and was showing him a picture of a girl in a bibbed dress worn over a blouse with puff sleeves. Oberdiah never found out if the girl was wife, fiancée, girl-friend or sister. At that moment — the rattle of machine-gun fire. Every soldier in No-Man's-Land threw himself down on the frozen ground.

The bullets came from the Allied trenches and kept coming at knee height. Lying flat, Oberdiah managed to get out from his tunic pocket a photograph of his own. This showed his parents and much younger sister standing in front of a country store. The road in front showed very white in the photograph for the few streets of his hometown were paved in quartz gravel. To one side of the store was a gumtree and on a hill behind the dark saw-tooth skyline of a pine plantation.

Beneath machine-gun bullets, Oberdiah held the photograph in front of the German's face. They again shook hands. Then each began the long flat crawl back to their own trenches.

The nights continued cold, with bright clear days. Each morning the Australians spread blankets, great-coats, even underclothes, across their wire. They were never shot at. Sunlight and warmth proved more effective than candleflame against *coodies* and for the first time in five months soldiers slept free of their bites.

Still they lived on jam-on-cheese — until some madcap remembered the cookhouse.

'Fritz'd never let us get away with that!'

'This jam-on-cheese's drivin' me crazy!'

'It's drivin' *me* sane! — Fritz's stopped firing. Why wouldn't he let us?'

'Because, Bonkers, it'd be such a perfect target no Fritz could resist it.'

'Livun' on jam-'n'-cheese — y' might as well be dead!'

It was decided to attempt locating and bringing up the mobile cookhouse. That took three nights. Those who brought it up also brought three sacks of food.

'We made a, er, requisition or two on the way.'

'Pity no quartermaster knows it.'

'Shh! — best part's this — not a tin o' jam or a round o' cheese among the lot o' it!'

In the morning dark, men stoked and lit the cookhouse fire. At first light they scattered as far from the cookhouse as they could, to watch its smoke go straight up into the blue.

None of the enemy's guns roared. Next morning the stoke-and-then-scatter was repeated. During that day and night men argued whether they would risk their first hot meal since coming to the trenches. At first light some were still arguing.

'Hey!'

A sentry's shout.

'Hey — cop a gander! Cop a gander at this!'

Men ran to the parapets. Then they were laughing, yelling, slapping each other's backs.

Behind the enemy trenchline, a ribbon of smoke rose straight up into the blue.

From then the Australians ate like kings! . . . Or so they said. Twice each day they lined up at the cookhouse for a huge tin bowl of porridge — no sugar and no milk — but with a thick slab of bacon on top and washed down with hot and strong black tea.

With the front trenches of that sector now so quiet, the Australians began receiving 'morale visits' from the brass. The troops were required to stand on their firing step as the contingent of brass passed. They would send off some high and wild shots above the enemy trenchline.

'That's it, Boys,' the Brass would shout, hurrying with heads down along the trenches. 'That's it — give it to 'em!'

Something similar must have been happening in the German trenches, for at times the length of the Australians' top row of sandbags would be ripped by machine-gun fire. A man with his head up would have been shot down — had there not been a dozen high warning shots first.

On different days when Oberdiah was standing in line to be served at the cookhouse, he nudged the soldier in front. Were he able to find the words, he'd have spoken. Instead he pointed to their cookhouse smoke going straight up, then across No-Man's-Land to where another ribbon of smoke rose into the blue. Grinning, he nodded. The soldier he'd nudged, grinned too. His eyes followed Oberdiah's point to the twin ribbons of smoke, and he too nodded. Then Oberdiah and the other soldier would both be nodding and laughing softly.

Following the visit of a top brass, there came an order directing that sector's howitzer back to reserve for rerifling. The guncrew were to return with their gun. A new gun would be sent up with its own crew.

Under cover of night the new gun arrived. This gun's mechanism was without backlash or slop, its barrel was unpitted, its rifling square-edged and sharp. And the new gun was matched by its crew: eighteen-year-olds whose boots and uniforms and hands were so clean. Who still had the tinge of Australian sun on their cheeks.

'Only thing that had me scared,' a newcomer said. 'Was that the war might be over before I got here!'

'Wait till The Hun gets a serve from our sixty-pounder!'

'It'll blast him clear out've his trenches!'

'Them Huns 'll be in Heaven -'

'Heaven? — Hell! That's where Huns go!'

Oberdiah said: 'We don't call him that.'

'Who?'

'Yair — who don't y' call what?'

'Him.' Oberdiah extended an arm in the direction of the German trenches. 'We call him Fritz.'

The guncrew laughed. They laughed and laughed.

Oberdiah had not thought what he'd said was funny, and the older soldiers were not laughing. The laughing guncrew made Oberdiah feel ridiculous. The more so as he now realized he had spoken in anger. And to complain of what the guncrew called Germans had not been what he had wanted to say at all.

But how to tell what he had intended to say? Less than a year previously, he had shouted phrases as strident as these barrack-room boastings. That less-than-a-year had unlearned for him both those phrases and that cast of mind. How could this guncrew be told an argument that had never been stated? Not even among the Australians themselves. And if it was stated, what chance of acceptance by this guncrew.

Another of the older troops told the guncrew to finish the rum themselves. Oberdiah and other older soldiers went out from what had become the guncrew's dugout.

Oberdiah considered what must be said should come from some rank higher than his own non-rank of Private. He went along the trenches to Jarven. Jarven was a Lance-Corporal.

'They've gotta be told,' Oberdiah said. 'Someone's gotta do it.'

Jarven agreed. 'Better see Hendricks.'

When he found Hendricks, Oberdiah repeated what he'd said to the Lance-Corporal. Sergeant Hendricks nodded.

Hendricks could not have been more emphatic.

'Believe you me they've gotta be told! They have to know.'

Yet he made no move toward the guncrew's dugout. After a time, he said: 'They seem t' me to be a bright-enough bunch. They'll twig to it. They're bright, all right — they'll twig to what's on without any of us having to open his mouth. They'll be right — believe you me they will!'

Oberdiah went to his dugout.

The sixty-pounder's roar wrenched him from sleep. He burst from his dugout — as the guncrew cheered.

Oberdiah was racing along duckboards as the guncrew cheered and cheered.

Then some words of the cheering burst upon him. As abruptly as he had commenced running, he stopped. He stood quite still.

Not until the cheerers had shouted themselves hoarse, did Oberdiah step up to a firing slot.

Back of the distant sandbag line, dark smoke spread like cloud where the ribbon of smoke used to be.

No one put their blankets and clothes out over the wire that day and none went near the cookhouse. There was no roar from German guns. Nor did the guns roar during the days that followed. After five days the cook again lit the cookhouse, and gradually men began standing in line with tin bowls and mugs.

Standing in line, Oberdiah turned toward the soldier behind him.

'Fritz would've known,' he said. 'He would have, wouldn't he?'

The soldier behind shrugged. Oberdiah nudged the soldier in front.

'He would have, surely. Fritz would've known we never meant it to happen!'

Ten days after the new gun came — on a bright chill morning with men standing in line and some with full bowls lingering beside the cookhouse for warmth — a gun roared. It roared three times.

When those who were able picked themselves up, there was no longer a cookhouse. Wounded and dying were strewn among burning and hissing rubble. Eight were dead. Another two were cut down by rifle fire when an attempt was made to take out the wounded during daylight.

So it was back to jam-on-cheese, back to *coodies*, back to shells exploding among the trenches and to shelling and sniping and taking out the wounded on a soldier's back at night.

That was the way it continued until the Australians were relieved by a French brigade. Then they walked out from these trenches, across the duckboards that zig-zagged across mud. They boarded omnibuses that took them north again to the valley of the Somme.

There Oberdiah, as other Australians, as almost all who fought on the Allied side, merged into one giant army. That army attacked, retreated across France, held, began an advance that took them into Belgium and, for some, into Germany itself.

When the war ended, Oberdiah Hobbs was in Belgium. For weeks he stood guard over prisoners whose return to their own homeland would not be celebrated by marching to tunes of glory.

He watched the prisoners file silently from the compound of barbed wire, to begin their long, machine-gun-guarded, march home. Then he boarded a convoy of one-time London omnibuses that took him the first leg of his journey home.

He soon had a prelude to his own return, for even on the unroofed topdecks of the omnibuses, men were singing.

As the convoy bumped over the cobblestone *pave* of Belgium, through villages and fields and again villages, women, old men and children, stood by doorways to wave. In one village, in front of a building standing solitary among rubble, a brass band of old men played with out-of-tune gusto in the rain.

For, of course, it was raining. Men sang as they huddled beneath the dripping downturned brims of their hats. The rain and the singing stopped when the convoy entered the outskirts of a town large enough to display the unroofed shell of a cathedral. There the convoy lurched to a stop.

Oberdiah stood to shake rain from his hat and greatcoat. That was when he saw, standing dark and central in the wet gleam of a cobble-paved square, the stone momument of a cross.

He stood staring. To be jerked from his feet as the convoy again started. Soon there was again rain and again singing. Oberdiah did not sing. He was held silent by the image of the cross now fixed in his mind.

That image was not held there by nostalgia for a faith once heard from the varnished pews of a country town church. In the hell through which he had lived, religious belief had been an early casualty. Nor was it in remembering a man standing as a cross in the centre of No-Man's-Land, though a shadow from that fell across his mind. It was as though he saw his own aspirations and knowledge forged in the years of war as a cross. The aspirations were fulfilled in that he was alive and returning to march between cheering and streamer-waving banks of his countrymen toward the joyful, tearful, hugs and handshakes of family and friends, to the backslaps and shouting in pubs, to a road that climbed as it would through a pine plantation until the pines ended abruptly and the road dipped to the country town of his youth with its trout streams and white quartz-gravel streets and its stories of gold.

But crossing the fulfillment of his hopes, fixed there in certainty and in pain, was his knowledge that across these celebrations of a public victory, lay a very private defeat.

Mother's Nose

Throughout the day cloud lay over the lake. With dusk coming on, the cloud lifted to reveal cloud-topped peaks mirrored without a ripple. Back from the shoreline the bush became fragrant with leatherwood and banksia, eucalypts and wattles. But an aroma more pungent — and welcome — than wet dripping bush came from the shore — the smell of wood smokily burning, of meat roasting.

There were six clustered around the fire, three couples I had met that day while hiking in these Tasmanian highlands. I was returning along a track from the carpark, carrying my contribution to their barbeque which I had been invited to share.

A cheer went up when I held out the bottle. After a confusion of, You first, and, No, no, after you — the brandy was accepted by a man of perhaps sixty years who in heavy accents and booming voice had earlier proclaimed himself an Abominable Lapman. He tipped the bottle, then passed it to his wife who he had boomingly pronounced an Abominable Lapwoman. From her it was passed to those doing the cooking, a couple whose accents declared them as Anglo-Australian as Aspros.

The third man of their party squatted back from the fire. As the bottle was held out to him, he stood, reached across the fire. For a moment he was enveloped in smoke from the damp burning wood and the roasting meat. There in the smoke with his arm outstretched, he swayed. His wife grabbed him. She pulled him back from the fire. She stood behind him, gripping his shoulders.

They stood like that for, perhaps, a minute. Then he shrugged off her hands, turned, strode to the water's edge and along the shore.

'Oh it is nothing — nothing at all.'

His wife's accent located her origins north of Glasgow.

'Give him a minute or two and he'll be — bonzer!'

She laughed at her own accent parodying that very very Australian word. We all laughed. Yet if her intention was for us to dismiss the incident with laughter — that was not the effect of her parody on me.

For already my curiosity had been stirred by her husband. He had not boomingly proclaimed his origins. Nor did his diction have any of his wife's rolling r's and hard c's. His speech was not quite Anglo-Australian — yet there was nothing about his diction identifiable as an accent. There was just something — a lilt, almost a lisp I had heard before and could not now place. It was precisely this inability to place him which awoke my curiosity.

I turned from the fire to follow him.

His wife touched my arm.

'He really will be . . . bonzer.'

She did not laugh this time; and I saw in her eyes it never had been a joke.

When I came to him he was sitting on a tree trunk that lay across the pebbly shore and into the lake.

'Are you all right?'

He had not turned at my approach, so it was the back of his head I addressed.

'I'm fine.'

'You looked as though you'd fall into the fire.'

'Well I didn't. And I'm all right.'

After a time, he turned. As though to apologize for the terseness of his replies, he said: 'It's just the smoke, the smell. Above all — the smell. It gets to me.'

He turned from me to gaze across the lake to mountains rising into cloud.

'Where were you from — originally?'

'Germany.'

He was short and dark-haired, tending to stockiness — none of these the once-lauded attributes of Aryans. His speech had none of the peculiarities of northern Germans speaking English: his th's did not veer toward the sound of d, nor his v's toward the sound of f. His dark hair and stocky build could pass for Bavarian, yet he had none of the Bavarian easy-going openness. Nor did he have the Cockney-like cheekiness of Berliners.

Abruptly he said: 'Mother is — always was — affected like that.'

He gave a quick grin, almost a guffaw, and added:

'Mother does everything by nose.'

I'd heard that before!

Once business had taken me far into East Germany and it was there, somewhere there . . . in . . . in . . .

'I'm from Saxony.'

Ahh!

Most languages have an equivalent expression. Ask an Indonesian peasant who has never seen a theodolite how he so precisely terraces a hillside for growing rice — he'll answer he knows it in his belly. Ask a Saxon the processes by which he came by an intuitive decision or act — unfailingly he'll answer he did it by nose.

I had heard that expression — spoken with just that lilt which is almost a lisp — not among countryside, nor in a village or town. I had heard it in one of the world's truly great cities. In -

'Dresden. You wanted to know where I came from originally — Dresden.'

His age would be, say, 38 — subtract from that the years since 1945 equals -

'You must have been in Dresden when it was bombed? You were there then?'

'So you know about that . . . Few Australians do. It was the greatest destruction of a city and its people in history. Greater than Hiroshima or Nagasaki — greater than the destruction of those two cities combined. No one knows how many were killed — the city was full of refugees fleeing the advance of Russian armies from the East. Some historians put the number who perished between ten o'clock one night and noon next day at a quarter of a million; some put the number as high as nine hundred thousand.

'However many — Mother, Father, Grandma and I would have perished too, if it hadn't been for Mother's nose.'

He swung his legs across the fallen tree trunk to face me. He leaned forward, elbows on knees, now eager to talk.

'Father was the opposite to Mother. Father calculated everything by slide-rule. He'd bought Mother the newest stove with a thermometer on the oven door and he proclaimed the superiority of cooking by exact temperature. Mother never looked at that thermometer — she smelled when a cake was to be taken out. Father berated the unscientific imprecision of her cooking — yet Mother was famous for her cherry shortcakes and strudels.

'At the beginning of the war Father quantified the resources, the manpower, the mechanization of each country, and he calculated how the war would end. He withdrew the family money from his savings account, converted it into gold. He had Mother make three canvas bags. In one he put the gold, share certificates and title deeds; in another, tins of food; the other, clothes.

'Toward the end of the war, Father made another calculation. The data for this he derived from putting the wireless and his head beneath the doona on his bed so he could listen to the B.B.C. without being overheard by people in the next flat. The Allied advance following the Normandy landing and the Russian armies swarming toward us from the East, convinced Father his earlier calculation was already confirmed. From that he reasoned since Berlin had been bombed to rubble and Hamburg had been destroyed by firebombing, Dresden — which never had been attacked — never would be.

'This calculation seemed proved when the anti-aircraft guns of Dresden were dismantled and trucked East to be used horizontally against Russian tanks. Such was his confidence he opened one of the bags and took out a long-denied luxury — a tin of ham. Mother took the tin back off him. She put the tin back in the bag and sewed it up. There was a great row about that. Father fumed at Mother for being incapable of seeing reason — the Allies were keeping Dresden to become the capital of conquered Germany. The heads in Berlin knew it — that's why the guns had been taken away. Dresden was the one German city that never would be bombed!'

Dusk had descended without any flare of sunset. The light had softened and deepened. Voices from those at the fire came to us as though from a great distance. No other sound broke the stillness, not even birds. There was no perceptible movement among foliage on the shore or on the surface of the lake.

'Though I was only four, I remember the bombing with such garish vividness that everything which has happened to me since seems indistinct, as though I have lived in the shadow of those fourteen hours.

'It was the night before the beginning of Lent, which was then a carnival night in Saxony. Mother and Father took me to the Grossen Garten to watch the skating, then I was brought home and put to bed much later than my usual bedtime.

'I don't recall if I was already asleep. What I remember vividly is that I was suddenly wide-eyed awake — the room was filled with dazzling light.

'I stood on the bed to look out the window, and saw the most beautiful yellow and green lights in the sky.

' "Mother — come and see!"

'I jumped from the bed, ran yelling to the kitchen.

' "Come and see the Christmas Trees in the sky!"

'The residential parts of Dresden were then all five- and six-storey blocks of apartments with a cellar beneath.

'Mother threw me into a pram which had been mine but for which I was too big, Father threw the three bags on top of me. Between them they carried the pram down flights of stairs. There were crumping sounds — distant, then near. The stairs rocked. Plaster and dust fell on us. The air raid sirens began wailing.

'People were doing as they had been instructed, they were streaming into the cellars. Father started down the steps into the cellar; but Mother — Mother's nose led her straight out into the street.

'Already incendiary bombs had set blocks of apartments aflame. Father yelled at Mother to come back. Come down into the cellar! Mother ran along the street, dragging after her the pram with me and the three bags in it.

'Father ran after her. High buildings on both sides of the street were in flames and the bitumen of the road was melting, bursting into flame. Father had to keep grabbing the pram, stopping Mother's rush so he could put out my hair which kept catching on fire.

'Mother was heading for her mother's house, which was a small detached two-storey house near the river. We reached it as the second wave of bombers came. They did not drop incendiary bombs: they dropped bombs that were purely percussive.

'As I came much later to know, the plan was to set the city ablaze and send people down into the cellars. Then for the second wave to topple the buildings, spreading the fires and sealing the cellars with rubble so the people in them would be baked or asphyxiated. It was a plan that worked to perfection.

'Mother bundled us all up stairs to the top storey. Suddenly — an immense thundercrack of sound. I was hurled out of the pram. Grandma was thrown across me. The floor lurched crazily downwards on one side, then on the other. I remember seeing Father rolling over and over across the floor.

'The whole ground floor had been obliterated and the top floor sat down where the ground floor had been. Father passed me out to Mother through what had been a wall. He scrambled around on the tilted and broken floor, found one bag and pointed out to Grandma another.

'So they were each carrying a bag and Mother carrying me as we ran through smoke. Mother was leading — often into streets blocked by fires or fallen buildings — but always toward the Marion Bridge across the River Elbe. This connected the Old Town part of Dresden where we lived to the New Town.

'Oil installations beside the Elbe had been hit, turning the river into a torrent of flames. Hurricane force winds generated by the firestorm which now enveloped the city, swept people over the railing of the bridge. Mother had Father, Grandma and herself lock arms around each other with me held in the middle. Like that we crept our way across the kilometer-long bridge.

'Mother was leading us to the one place in the city impregnable to bombs. This was a railway station in the New Town part of the city.

'Inside the two arched entrances was an open area of shops and ticket-selling offices under a high domed glass roof. Going off from this were corridors that went underground connecting to the platforms and to the cloakrooms, restaurants, baggage rooms and toilets.

'People were streaming into these underground corridors. Keeping pressed together, we pushed our way into one. There Father proclaimed no bomb could penetrate the concrete and earth and station platforms above — we were safe at last. Mother pushed on. Holding me, she forced her way between people then exorted Father and Grandma to keep with her. Mother reached a door — the mens toilet. Inside were fewer people but even there Mother kept right on. She opened a door to one of the cubicles and got us all in.

'Throughout the night and morning the four of us stayed in that one metre by one metre toilet. There were distant crumping sounds and close thundercracks of sound. Once we were all thrown against one wall and cement and dust rained down on us. There was smoke, the smell of burning. Screams. Thudding and thudding and thudding against the door of the toilet cubicle. For a time Grandma was sitting on the toilet seat, holding me; and in the darkness I saw white fingers and knuckles over the top of the door. Then Mother was holding me and I looked again for the white fingers and knuckles but they were gone.

'There in the darkness, Father made a discovery. The bag Grandma had brought was not, as he'd supposed, the one with the gold and the share certificates. He had the one with clothes, she the one with tins of food.'

While he spoke, he had stood and he made short karate-chop gestures.

As the light had faded, the clouds lifted from the mountains. A single pale wash of sunset silhouetted the Western peaks, one ridge a perfect unbroken slope to the domed crest.

'It was long after all sound outside had ceased, that Father got Grandma and Mother to stand on the toilet seat so he could open the door. When he did — bodies fell in on us.

'He had to lift and push aside the bodies, and we all climbed over others to get out. Against the farther wall from the cubicles, bodies in a pile sloped almost to the ceiling.

'In the crush of people pushing their way in, people against the cubicles and walls had been trampled down, then those who stood on them were pushed down, trampled, then those who trampled them had in turn been trampled.

'Along the walls of the corridors were more bodies. The corridors now opened out on — rubble. Where the high domed roof had been, could now be seen the smoke-filled sky.

'We coughed, gagging on the dense smoke and the heavy roasting smell. We did not go out either of the two arched doorways — there was no longer any front wall to the station.

'In the whirling smoke Father spoke to a man who said the Marion Bridge was gone but he had been able to cross at the Friedrich Bridge. Father said Grandma's house was destroyed though not burnt when we fled it. It might not have burned. All the family now owned was in the other bag and he just might be able to find it. He told Mother to take Grandma and me as far as the Friede Forest and wait for him there.

'Mother grabbed his arm, imploring him not to go. The bridge would be unsafe — he would get caught up in the fire — he would choke to death on the smoke — the bombers would come again.

' "For what would the bombers come?" There in the smoke Father tried to reason with Mother. "The city is already destroyed."

'Grandma cried out. She was pointing up. Above the dense whirling smoke were bombers — hundreds of bombers. As we watched, the first rows of bombers climbed higher then came down in a bombing run.

'They dropped incendiary bombs onto what was already an inferno.'

From the fire a voice called that if we didn't hurry to tucker — there wouldn't be any.

We walked along the pebbly shore. The smell of smoke and roasting meat came to us.

'I remember the sound of Mother's breath rasping in her throat as she ran. We ran, we stumbled, we walked all that day without ever getting beyond the smoke and the smell. That night there was no darkness. Though we were now many kilometers away, the farmlands and forest and the road ahead were lit by the hellish light of the burning city.'

The Abominable Lapman held out to each of us a steak on a plate. The man who had survived Dresden ignored the meat. He took the plate of salad and a bread roll his wife had for him. I took across the bottle and he tipped it quickly then passed it back. I offered it to his wife, but she shook her head. So I stood with the bottle in one hand and steak on a plate in the other — not eating, not drinking.

He gave that quick grin which was almost a guffaw.

'Sometimes I get a feeling, an emotion, which overwhelms me. It is as though in a few seconds I live through it all again. It's not my dreams that do that to me, not my psyche, not my imagination or memory. But if I catch a smell . . . of wood burning . . . smoke . . . the smell of meat roasting . . .'

'It is his nose,' his wife, with her Scottish accent, said. 'He gets that from his mother.'

A Burgomaster's Story

It was near midnight and we had walked past the shop windows of the silent town and were crossing a park that lay between the hotel where we had eaten together, and the one at which we were both staying.

'Men of my age in your country have known war,' he said. 'But they could not have known it as we did: they went *away* to war — in Europe the war came to us. You come from a country that has never been occupied by foreign troops; you could not know what that does to people. I will tell you one man's experience of what it was like.'

He was a plump Dutch-Jewish businessman who had arrived to visit a factory in this central Swedish town on the same day as myself.

As he was speaking, we arrived at a fountain floodlit in the centre of the park, and stopped to gaze up at the tumbling water.

'You are young,' he said. 'I am not young. I would like to sit a while.'

The hotel — and bed — was just the other side of the park; and the previous night I had caught the midnight train from Copenhagen, then changed trains at four in the morning.

'Come-on, come-on — sit,' he said. 'Sit — and I will tell you.'

Not only was I tired, I was also cold. There was a mist coming in from the lake just beyond the park, the shops, the railway station. But . . . I sat.

'In Holland the war came with the German High Command announcing they would bomb our cities, one after the other. It seems hardly to be believed, now, but we thought they were bluffing — cities are not military targets! Then the bombing of Rotterdam . . . Within five days our army surrendered; the occupation of our country began. Only the underground fought on. Hitler himself was later to say that the Dutch army fought for five days and was defeated, but the Dutch underground fought more than five years and was never defeated.

'And I . . .?

'As the occupation commenced, I closed my business, sent my two boys to different parts of the country under changed names and my wife to Amsterdam with still another name; my own name also changed. Most Jews did nothing. Many thought what they had heard had happened in Germany to be propaganda of the Left! There were a hundred thousand Jews in Holland at the beginning of the occupation; at its end, seven thousand. My parents, I lost. My wife's parents. Her brothers. Two of my . . . But the list would take until morning.

'I became drafted into a labour camp. Not as a Jew — no, that was not recognised — but as an able-bodied man. I lived in terror that my identity be discovered. Never did I know what had happened to my family, as we were carted like cattle in trucks from one part of Holland to another; sleeping in barracks when we were lucky, or on bare boards, or the ground; living and sleeping in what began as a uniform and became rags; always hungry; always among rubble, rubble from the bombed bridges and buildings we cleared and rebuilt, rubble that we carted away so that runways could be rebuilt for German planes, among rubble we dug graves . . .

'For two years I was a part of that labour gang.

'Then one day, as we were clearing away from a bridge damaged by Allied bombing, a German officer we had not seen before came to where we were working. Unlike the others, he was not interested in the amount of damage. In our speed of clearing away he was not interested. In what was he interested? In us, it seemed; for he walked among us asking each in turn about their life before the occupation. I found excuses to work as far from him as I could. But what I dreaded, happened. He sent a guard to bring me to him. There I looked down at his polished boots and his clean and pressed uniform, then up into his face, at the hard grey eyes and the faintest of smiles; and in that instant I saw that — he *knew*.

'He commanded I follow him to his car.

'This, I thought, is the way it ends.

'His chauffeur was dozing at the wheel, and we stood beside the car while he questioned me about myself. I told him I had had my own import and wholesale business, which was true — though I lied as to where my business had been situated, what I imported and from where — that I had been president of a wholesalers' association — also true — and that I was a widower, which, I fervently hoped, was not.

'Even after his questions and my answers he made no mention of my race. He told me he was military commandant of a town on the River Maas, in charge of a holding force there. The river at that point is over three kilometers wide; and the far bank was occupied by the Allies. What he needed was a burgomaster to conduct the civil administration of the town. Someone, he added significantly, someone reliable.

'And so he had chosen a Jew! One mistake, one little slip, and -

'What, I asked, had happened to the elected burgomaster? Was he not . . . reliable?

'Oh he had been reliable. Most reliable. He had co-operated with the occupying forces in every way. They could not have had a more reliable man.

'What, I insisted, had happened?

'People he had lived among all his life began to despise him for being so helpful. The townspeople drove him to it. He had hanged himself.

At this point of his telling, my companion stood and began slowly pacing from the circle of light surrounding the fountain, into the abrupt dark. I quickly joined him along the path that wound between dark banks of shrubbery, towards the lights of the hotel.

'So I was taken from the rags and sleeping on boards or beneath trucks and the hunger of the labour gang, to a room in the town hall itself, a tailored-to-measure suit and three shirts, a woman coming each day to clean and cook. And food! For weeks all I wanted was to eat and eat and eat.

'Eating, in fact, became a kind of consolation. For when I walked the streets, people turned their backs to me. Toughs spat when I passed. People who had come to my office with requests that morning, in the afternoon crossed the street at my approach. Children were schooled to call after me. Puhl's *puppe*, they jeered. Puhl's puppet . . .

'Each morning Commandant Puhl received me and we drank coffee while we discussed the day-to-day running of the town, and he countersigned each of the written directives I was required to give. Every detail was administered in this way. Nothing was permitted to happen in that town without the approval of his signature.

'Yet there were times I was grateful for those morning conversations and coffee: in spite of the never-mentioned, but never-for-a-moment forgotten, threat, the commandant was at least civil to me. And there were times when the threat seemed preferable to the derision of the streets, that had driven my predecessor to hang himself.

'Yet would those townspeople, I wonder, have turned their backs, crossed the street, spat, had they known that the most swaggering tough — the one who spat on my shoes then bumped me, to the approval of watching townspeople and even of passing

German soldiers — beneath cover of that bump, slipped into my hand a folded scrap of paper? Would they have sent their children jeering after me, had they known on that paper was written the assumed name, fabricated life-history and business of a pilot or gunner shot down during a night raid and now being smuggled back to England and to other night flights over Europe?

'You see, the Dutch underground's whole system for returning flyers to England focused on that town; or, rather, on the town's ferry, which continued operating right through the war. Three kilometers across the River Maas and the pilots were in Allied occupied Holland. But how heavily fenced and guarded, floodlit and patrolled, was the ferry's berth! How well-lit and patrolled were the banks! How thoroughly checked was each person's papers who crossed on the ferry!

'That the flyer's papers could withstand checking was the underground's job; that they had a written, signed and counter-signed directive to cross, was mine.

'I am not by nature a reckless or courageous man. Six hundred years my family can trace its history in Holland, all careful Dutch-Jewish merchants: unfertile ground for the production of heroes. And even the deeds themselves lacked any of the dash or style of heroics.

'After receiving the assumed name, assumed business and actual date of crossing, I wrote the directive and inserted it with others to be presented for countersigning next morning. How I fiddled and shuffled the papers, placing *that* directive first third from the top, then second from the bottom, then in the middle! How I practised for hours — whole nights! — the exact actions with which the directives would be passed to the commandant and the casual — so-o-o-o casual — movement of wrist and fingers which spread the pile of directives so that just the line for his signature was visible on each paper, one below the other. How I rehearsed the story or joke or business of the day with which to distract him while he signed.

'That would be a night of no sleep for me. Then the morning, and my hands shaking so that again and again I cut myself shaving. Food I could not eat. My stomach twisted into a hard knot that the hours I spent in the toilet did nothing to loosen. Had I been a practicing Jew, I would have prayed in that toilet — but in God and Divine Help I do not believe. I believe in adrenalin. *How* I believe in adrenalin! For when I at last stood before Commandant Puhl's desk, with what steady hand and so casual a gesture I tossed — yes, tossed! — the directives onto his desk and with such off-handed movement spread them for him to sign. And how expansively I told him a story! How he laughed! "Willem," he would say, "you're unusually gay this morning." Laughing, as he signed. And signed. And signed . . .

'But do not for a moment think that after such tension you can then calmly go about your business. Oh, no! The adrenalin racing and bubbling in your veins and you are as though floating — high! — crazy! — reckless! — and mad, utterly mad. Then I was my own enemy — when I could have given myself and the whole Dutch underground away with a laugh!

'I am not usually a drinking man; but for those times I hoarded brandy, schnapps — anything! — in my room. Alone and behind a locked door I would drink until I had drugged myself into a sleep that lasted twelve, thirteen, even fifteen hours. Then to awake; sick; and limbs as though of lead; and if for a moment came any thought or feeling of relief that now it was over, at its heels came the certain knowledge that that day, or the next, in a week's time or a fortnight's, in the middle of being jeered at in the street, a folded slip of paper would be passed to me, and it would begin all over again . . .'

The next morning the Dutch business man and I breakfasted together. We sat at a table by the window of the first floor dining room, and looked down at the glints of sunlight on the wind-whipped surface of the lake. For a long time we were silent.

'What I told you last night,' he then said, 'all happened a long time ago. And after we parted, I went to my room and asked myself why I had told you. It is a time I want only to forget. The day the war ended was the day I left that town (I have never been back) and began searching for my wife, and finding her — thin! so thin, but with legs horribly swollen — then nursing her back to health. Later began the search that eventually found my two boys.

'We had all lived through that time and never speak of it, wanting only to forget.

'But then we had a daughter. Our Child of Peace, we call her among ourselves. And often she came to ask me about the war, and I would tell her only that it was something to forget, not to be kept in memory by telling.

'And perhaps that is why I told you: someone from her side of youth, and from a country knowing little more of what it was like than she.

'For now she, our Child of Peace, is engaged to be married. And some days before I left to come here, she came to me, saying, "Pappa, Leon's father fought in the war. He was a pilot. Three times he was shot down and escaped back to England and flew again. What did you do in the war, Pappa? What?"

'And I looked at my Child of Peace, my princess, and in her eyes I saw what she wanted me to say. That I also had been a helmeted avenger swooping out of the night sky among searchlight beams and flack and explosions and the cannon fire and anti-aircraft bullets rattling and ripping through wings and fuselage. *That* kind of bravery she could understand.

' "What, Pappa?" she said. "What did you do?"

' "I . . .?" I said, and already I could see her frown as she prepared to accept that she could never boast of me as Leon could of his father.

' "But you must have done *some*thing!"

'Already she has accepted her humiliation, and is impatient to be gone from me.

' "I . . .?" I said, "I was a burgomaster." '

Crap Route Through Austria

Wishing Erica Luschen and myself luck on our attempt to reach the Loser peak, Mr Sleusch settled himself on a bench outside the wooden hut. He would start back down the mountain in three hours; an hour, he calculated, before we began our descent from the peak.

We left him there, in warm sunbright; and soon we came to the first patches of snow. Higher, now, than the highest spires of fir, ahead, jutting above the snow, only rocks and a trunkless relative of the fir called *Latschen* — lying fir.

Soon neither rock nor lying fir showed as we sank to our knees, crawling in places, in the soft spring snow. Then we sank to our waists, each taking turns to stamp down snow in order to flounder forward.

I was paying for all-night sessions of beer and brandy and schnapps during trade fairs and visits to trade acquaintances at factories in Hannover and Frankfurt, Hamburg, Nuremburg, Passau, Linz. The exertion of stamping down snow caused me to sweat from every pore. A moment's pause in this exertion and the sweat froze against my skin.

That morning I had begun the climb with the athletic Erica Luschen and Mr Sleusch. His intention to reach the Loser hut; her's, the summit.

Mr Sleusch proved very fit for his seventy-plus years; though often Erica Luschen and I would outdistance him, and then sit talking as we waited for him to tack and veer his way up the slope to us. During one of these waits, she told me she had once been married and was not now.

'In Australia,' she asked, 'you are married — yes?'

When I told her, she said:

'Oh well, Australia is very far away.'

That had been when I decided not to stay at the hut with Mr Sleusch; but to attempt the summit with Erica Luschen.

The climb in snow seemed interminable. Then there was cloud. Later, *much* later, there was rock beneath our boots, and soon snow gave way to a dome of rock swept free of snow by the wind. Here density of cloud and the cold were intense. With arms around each other, we stumbled through cloud toward the iron cross marking the summit.

Kissing the cross, we then kissed each other.

Then began our stumbling, scrambling, fumbling descent. Arms around each other, we rolled in snow. Laughing at our own mad tangle of limbs.

'I had not asked,' she said. 'How long you are staying at the village.'

'A week. A full week before I go to a trade fair in Milan.'

'And I — another four days. Five nights.'

Australia, I thought, is very far away.

When I'd told a German trade-cronie the way I was going, he said: 'Start further north so you can get on board the Trans Europe Express through the Tyrol — then you'll *really* see something. You can sit up in the topdeck observation car, sloshing booze. That way you're going, it's the crap route.'

Business, however, made it imperative I go south to Passau, then across the Austrian border to Linz. A night in that city's all-night bars with a hard-drinking factory manager, expelled any further craving for sloshing booze. And the train in which next day I was travelling did not have a bar, it did not have an observation car; it could not have been more at odds with the Trans Europe Express.

It was just two connected carriages with (Austrian Railways be praised!) a toilet in the middle.

School-girls and -boys got on at one village, off at the next; peasant women wearing dirndles and boots with laces hooked into clips and carrying steel-spiked walking sticks, got on with loaded baskets, then off at the next station or the next, as the train meandered past lakes, mountains, villages, of rural Austria.

The scenery chiefly admired by me, however, was the polished wood panelling back of the toilet door.

The train guard (solitary constant on the train beside myself) observed my goings and goings and goings to view the wood panelling, with a sympathy and sense of being host that induced him constantly to attempt conversation. With his English no better than my German, the effort this required caused my inner voice to wish upon his sympathy death by what my stomach was giving me. It took half an hour for me to comprehend a single question about Australia (of where, I came to understand, he and his children had seen a television program), and him to comprehend my answer. Following yet another visit to view the wood panelling, he was waiting for me. Beaming, he stood at rigid attention and in word perfect English sang to me — *Skippy The Bush Kangaroo*.

And the trials of the train journey were but a prelude to the trials of that night in a mountain village inn. I assaulted my still recalcitrant stomach with venison steaks served with whipped cream and noodles and baked pears. Only to discover just *how* recalcitrant my stomach could be.

Opening wooden shutters on sunlight glinting on the fir-margined lake and peaks wimpled with snow, brought little radiance to my morning.

Avoiding breakfast at the inn, I bought dry bread rolls at a village shop then wandered the cobble-paved road past shops with latticed windows and houses with antlers over doorways.

Where the cobblestones ended and a walking track went on, was the cemetery. This was not at all a cheerless place. Each grave was a miniature garden with pansies, tulips and mountain flowers in bloom. Jars of narcissus and edelweiss were placed either side of each intricate filigree of iron forming a cross. Often there was a photograph beneath glass at the centre of the cross; and always, central at the base, was a thick coloured candle. On some graves the candle was sheltered by being placed between the cross and the jar of flowers, on others the candle was within a metal frame supporting coloured glass.

I was on the track past the cemetery, when I was overtaken by a woman of my own mid-thirty years and a man who was short and spare and who might have been her father.

The woman greeted me in German. At the stiltedness of my reply, she switched to English.

'So — you are also today to climb the Loser?'

I explained I intended that day only to walk the ten-kilometer circumference of the lake.

'Oh well, our way is together for maybe two-three kilometer.'

I fell into step beside them. The man, I discovered, was not her father at all; nor were they of the same nationality. He was Austrian, she from northern Germany. They met while staying at the same guest house, one specializing in health meals, where carrot-juice, celery-juice and buttermilk are served in place of beer and wines.

This was imparted to me by the woman. The man attempted conversation; but after a phrase or two in English, that language failed him. He smiled apologetically, then continued in German which the woman translated for me. He had learnt English at school, but that was very long ago. Today was his seventy-second birthday. On his twenty-first birthday he had been holidaying at the same village, and on that one day he had both met his future wife and had climbed to the summit of the Loser. During the years since, he had kept fit by exercising every day, and he drank beer only on holidays.

As for his wife, she was still alive and staying with him at the guest house. She now had trouble walking and could only manage a few metres before having to rest.

He knew he would not be able, this day, to climb right to the summit. If he reached as far as the Loser Hut and picked flowers at the hut to take to his wife, this would be for him a wonderful day.

The woman was also devoted to fitness. Her work-a-day week included jogging, gymnasium, squash. During the two weeks she had been holidaying at the village, she followed a regimen of exercises, runs, walks and set rest periods. Her attempt to climb the Loser was, she said, an examination of her fitness program.

We reached where one track went on around the lake and another went up the hillside. That was when she told me she had been married once and was not now.

'So — we go our different ways. — Yes?'

That *yes*? turned statement into a question; just as her fixed gaze turned her smile into a challenge.

I looked at the track beside the tranquil lake, then at the steep climb over rocks and between trunks of beech and fir. I looked back at the challenging half-smile — and began to climb.

There were handshakes, introductions; though little conversation: our breath had to be reserved for the climb.

Only when we all stopped to rest, or when Erica Luschen and I waited for Mr Sleusch, was there a chance for conversation.

I was grateful for those rests. Though in Australia I had hiked with my wife over the Victorian Alps and

Tasmania's mountains, three weeks in Europe had robbed me of much fitness. That was good German beer, Rhineland Moselle, brandy and *schnapps* I was sweating from every pore.

While we rested, Mr Sleusch would tell of his life. Via Erica Luschen's translation, he related he had worked from age seventeen to seventy in the Customs Department of the Austrian Railways. During early years of marriage, he and his wife had for many years gone without holidays so that they could save for their children's education. One son had been killed in the last war; the other son was a teacher who had once studied at Cambridge. Their daughter had become a doctor.

Mr Sleusch wanted to know about my wife and children. I was uncomfortable at this questioning, the more so as it came via Erica Luschen's translation. I saw her smile at the shortness of my replies.

Past midday, we arrived at the Loser Hut. Erica Luschen and Mr Sleusch each ate the lunch they had brought; I ate a dry bread roll, thankful the one eaten earlier was still where it was intended. She shared with me one of two bottles of carrot juice she had brought. Mr Sleusch had a litre of buttermilk. He did not unscrew the screw-top bottle because, he said, he was hot from the climb and the milk might upset his stomach.

Then he settled himself on the wooden bench. We began the climb.

The sun was already down when Erica Luschen and I saw Mr Sleusch below us on the track, picking his way among rocks and trunks of fir.

When we reached him, we saw he was carrying flowers arranged in a neat bunch. He was avid to hear of our climb, nodding in recollection of his own climb in spring snow. When he climbed, there had been no cloud and the view — he could still remember the view!

Dusk was coming on when we came to a flat open space. Here Mr Sleusch proposed we sit. Erica Luschen and I sat — Mr Sleusch did not.

Standing, he swept an arm around to include, as though in embrace, the mountains and the woods, the glade, our being here together.

'*Alles*,' he said. '*Alles ist gute*.'

Then he began a quite formal speech — in English. His English lapsing in German only when what so plainly he had rehearsed in his mind failed him. He said he had twice lived through years of war, losing his father in one war and one son in another. He'd seen Austrians fighting alongside Germans and against Germans and against each other, and Australians had come very far to fight against Germans and against some Austrians; yet here we were together on a day of great happiness for him, in this place where everything is good.

He repeated that last phrase in English, then finished as he'd begun.

'*Alle ist gute*.'

Erica had taken out her remaining bottle of carrot juice. She held it up to salute Mr Sleusch's speech, and she drank. She was about to pass the bottle to me, when Mr Sleusch insisted — emphatically insisted — I take his drink. I unscrewed the previously unopened bottle — and inhaled a rancid whiff.

With bottle half way to lips, I knew what Mr Sleusch did not: what bumping up the mountain and down in his haversack had done to the milk.

I looked up at Mr Sleusch so courteously wishing to share with us his happiness, so expansively indicating the three of us and the mountains, the woods, this glade — and I saw more. I saw the manifest goodness of Mr Sleusch's life.

I held the bottle high to salute him. Then I tipped the bottle and began chewing, gulping down, chewing and gulping the rancid cheesey curds and the whey. I kept on until I had the whole litre down.

It was dark when we reached the cemetery. Here Mr Sleusch shook my hand and hurried away — he had flowers for his wife and a day — such a day! — to tell her about.

Erica Luschen and I stood by the rock wall surrounding the cemetery. Now all the candles were alight. Flickering and bristling light from candles took colour from tulips or pansies or the coloured glass panels of lamps. Women moved among the graves, calling to each other as they stooped to plant a flower or replace narcissus in a jar.

From the hill behind came first one tinkle of cow bell. Then another. And another and another and another.

'Who would think,' Erica Luschen said, 'that a cemetery could be such a romantic place. Yes?'

Yes, a romantic place.

Yet we stood without touching. Once I began to say . . . something . . . Something that hung unfinished between us.

The women all left the cemetery. Cow bells now came not from the hill behind, but from within the village.

With a stiff and quite formal handshake, she left me there. We had not arranged to meet again. Nor would we.

I watched her leave the close darkness where we had stood together beside the cemetery wall, watched her pick her way between flickering coloured lights and into the further darkness.

Ooooooh, those rancid cheesey curds reacting and reacting and reacting inside of me.

'*Alles*,' I said, quite loud, into the close darkness that surrounded me. Then louder still, trying, trying, to recapture the exact intonation and accent of Mr Sleusch:

'*Alles. Alles ist gute.*'

The Suppliant

For a one-time believer become estranged, the Church prescribes he kneel — then believe. A rational man, surely, would reverse the prescription, requiring decision first, then the deed; and insist the prescribed order reveals merely the suppliant's will. Yet by this illogic might an unsure painter draw his first charcoal strokes, by this tenet might a writer start a story.

For Rodney Hallens — driving, the needle towards a hundred and twenty, the bitumen ahead quite straight between scattered gums — rationality had been his polestar. Yet since his return to people and places that chafed with their familiarity, the decision whether or not to again leave the familiar had become a search for a symbol or sign that would present the decision ready-made and unequivocal to him.

We would see a sign a poet had lamented, and he sought one. Specifically, at the moment, a road sign. But the pointed direction assumed in his mind transatlantic proportions: a sign that might point the future direction of his life.

A sign-post ahead, and he eased his foot on the accelerator. But it was miles yet to his sign. He sped on. To his left a gum-strewn plain; but on his right there increasingly rose above the red sandy ground and gums, a range of craggy shoulders and hips of naked rock.

A different range, this, to those he had gone walking in half a year before. There he had followed roads that climbed and elbow-turned beside tumble-and-swirl streams, past houses with antlers over doorways and cow pastures called *Blaa-alm*; then leaving the road to climb the track that brought him above the tree-line, to see the glacier on the Dachstein suspended in the sky, and below, the village, dotted and blocked beside the perfect pear shape of the lake.

His memories of Europe were all like that: chocolate box tableaus of fir and deer-antler and snow, or of an *Openhaus* with marble steps and statues, or of artists painting at easles among the sidewalk throng.

His stay in Europe had been a dream exceeded.

This European dream had grown out of his awakening from another. This first dream had been of his own country rising at last out of its cat-o'-nine-tails and English-overlord past to become uniquely itself. His reading, visits to one-time convict cells, dumps of gold and copper-mines, his notebooks in which he recorded the accents and phrases with which old people told of the past, had become the material out of which he fashioned stories and plays of his country's past. Magazine and stage-stories that were celebrations of the heroic.

But what could rise heroically out of the clipped lawns and pruned roses of suburban streets, the macadam, carbon-monoxide and chrome of the highways?

That something heroic and unique could rise, he had held no doubt. And had counted himself a volunteer among those who worked to make it happen.

He had been woken from that dream by the sound of police boots kicking into a felled demonstrator during the Johnston visit. And hearing cabinet ministers braying hoarse with denunciations of demonstrations against the war to be flagrant lawlessness on our streets.

The south-east Asian wars had been one part of his awakening; the disintegration of his marriage had been the other.

His marriage to Victoria had commenced with a honeymoon on the Queensland coast. Then year following year they'd returned to walk far out on the mudflats at low tide. Days were spent fishing from the beach; nights in playing cards with people from the caravan park or holiday flats; and to clinging and panting together in the warm nights.

This life of shared hedonism came in time to be blown away by the smallest of puffs: squabbles over the TV programs she watched, her resentment that he would again be writing for hours, or at yet another meeting or march or demonstration. In the end they sold the house and split the surprisingly little they had to show for their eight years together.

Victoria was going north to the coastal town of their holidays. She had arranged lease of a shop there and was confident she could make a living selling to tourists and to people from the caravan park opposite.

Victoria delayed her own drive north until the day he left for Europe. In what had previously been his car, she drove him to the airport. They sat in the car park. Each, at first, made attempts at conversation. Then they sat without speaking. They shook hands. Neither attempted a kiss.

His disenchantment with his marriage and his country had become linked in his mind as the public and private faces of the same thing. So as the plane took to the air and he saw the coastline slip behind, it seemed symbolic to him that he had left both on the same day.

After his slow awakening from one dream, he dived from the sky into another.

He prowled London streets with a satchel of plays under arm and a street guide in hand, searching out backstreet playhouses where he left copies of his plays. He left manuscripts of stories on editors' desks, being able to remind one editor of a story previously published by his magazine.

On his second morning in London, he rang

Michael Bruthern. Bruthern converted novels into playscripts for British television.

The pub in which they met was the one pub in London (Bruthern pronounced) where you could get a Carlton and United icy cold. The bar was crowded with Australians. Not the place, Hallens reflected, to plead that cold beer gave him bladder trouble.

His bladder was still painful next day when Bruthern introduced him to a television producer. The producer scanned an offered script, pronounced it competent, though far too Australian. He stated that later in the year they would be embarking on a series of European Classics. Previously they had done *Madame Bovary* and *The Idiot*. The producer suggested Hallen make his own selection, do a précis of, say, ten episodes, and a pilot script of the first episode. Nothing promised, the producer said, but, wel-l-l-l, we'll see . . .

Elated at not having to immediately set to work, Hallens stayed another week, endured another bladder-aching session of the amber fluid, told Bruthern he would return in about three months when his money would have run low, then boarded a plane for Hannover.

If London had been an up-tempo version of a world he already knew, Hannover was his introduction to what might well have been another planet.

His first aerial glimpse, was of ancient three-tiered barns and triple-storeyed farm buildings squatting among flat green fields. Then, feet-on-the-ground, he stared at men in peaked caps and overcoats riding bicycles beneath bare branches of linden and birch under soft grey skies.

In this mystic world the theatres he attended were not the cramped back street playhouses of London, but giant *Openhausen* where doormen in tails ushered you to even the cheapest seats. Here, too, was an open-air stage in palace gardens where a row of gilt statues formed the backdrop. There a season of open air theatre began in June, so he pencil-marked the program and altered his plans so as to return for performances of Moliére and Brecht and Shakespeare.

Then from train windows he glimpsed castles veiled in rain and deer seen in the early-morning half-light; he walked beneath linden trees in northern deer-parks and in Austria climbed among rocks and snow and the mountain lying fir; at sidewalk stalls he ate herring in rolls, smoked salmon in rolls, and drank *bier* that was warm, frothy, and kind to his bladder. On railway platforms and in carriages and *pensione* rooms he read novels by Tolstoy and Turgenev and Flaubert, and made tentative divisions of each into episodes.

By then the shape of his own future had presented itself sharp-edged and primary-coloured to him. He would live and work, say, nine months of each year in London; then three months of each year in Europe. Any likelihood of returning to Australia did not appear in this possible future at all.

He was in Milan, visiting prescribed galleries, and had returned to his box-sized room after a morning that included Leonardo's *Last Supper*, when the proprietor handed him a package. He sat on the bed and opened it to find inside a letter from Bruthern, and a sealed envelope with an Australian postmark.

Though the second letter intrigued him the more, he read the first. Bruthern wrote that while none of the London playhouses expressed interest in his plays, a theatre in Leeds was impressed to the point of almost certainly putting on one of his plays in July or August. Would he be able to be present during rehearsals?

The second letter was typewritten and as terse as a telegram:

Rod

Vicki's stacked your car and in hospital. The

Holden's a write-off and Vicki damn-near. On Intensive Care list. If she gets over concussion etc she'll be in traction for months. Shop's shut. Rent and wholesalers' bills still to be paid and bank low. Don't let a little thing like this spoil your gadding about. No love

Val.

His youngest sister had never accepted his marriage to Victoria was finished. On re-reading the letter, he felt the barb go in. He left the room to walk the crowded footpaths, apologizing to people he kept bumping and finding himself at corners without any idea of which way to turn. He became hungry and bought cassata but later found he was still holding the now soggy cone and the cassata melted in pink and green dribbles over his wrist and down his sleeve. Later that night, he was first sarcastic, then bullying, to the man who answered the 'phone at the airport terminal.

Along the Queensland coast Summer had continued through the months of Autumn without a glimpse of the sun-routed season. Holiday flats bordering the esplanade and the foreshore caravan park continued full in May. Though mackerel began their run up the coast on-calender, the winter whiting refused to appear.

Rodney Hallens twice put down his cases and tried to arrange his coat on top of one of them as he walked the esplanade footpath. The second time was outside Victoria's shop. He stood sweating, as he peered through locked glass doors at the rows of groceries behind counters, the deep freeze, card racks, fishing rods, reels and lines arranged in a corner. Though he held the key, he pushed arms into coat sleeves and carried the cases around the corner at the restaurant next door; then two blocks along and up stairs to Victoria's second storey flat.

Plane, train, bus and taxi had finally discharged him at the Harcourt Bay Hospital an hour and a half previously. Mrs Hallens, he had been told, was now out of Intensive Care. She was in Ward Three. Yes, he could go up.

Ward Three was really a balcony enclosed by high, vertical, aluminium louvres that could be opened, angled and shut. Victoria lay with one leg bare from the knee raised in traction. He saw her eyes open wide on seeing him, then she closed them. She said he might at least have given her warning.

For an hour he sat beside the bed, trying not to stare at the stainless steel pin to which weights were attached that protruded each side of her shin. He made the bantering remarks he had prepared during the thirty hour plane flight; then they sat, not so much conversing as each offering phrases then waiting and watching to see if the other accepted.

On subsequent visits that tentative note remained. Only when discussing pricing or ordering or the takings for the day did they regard themselves on neutral ground.

Each day he opened the shop at eight, took delivery of bread and milk, then swept the floor and the footpath outside. At first he had taken an exercise book, pencils and thesaurus, for he had definitely decided upon Flaubert's *Sentimental Education* as the European Classic to be adapted for television. However, whenever the trickle of customers ceased, recollection of the last figure in the shop's bank balance goaded him into cleaning and rearranging showcards and packets of cereal on shelves, and showcards, rods and reels in the window.

Soon he took to setting the alarm at five each morning, then working until precisely seven-fifteen, before breakfasting and walking to the shop.

On his first full day there, he closed the shop at six, crossed the esplanade to the beach. He stood watching a girl of, perhaps, seventeen, standing thigh-deep in the foam and green of the full tide, fishing. She wore a maroon tee-shirt above her bikini bottom; her face and limbs were deeply tanned and her hair hung black and free to between her shoulders. Her bosom was slight but her thighs and hips were firm and full. In his notebook he wrote she had nothing of prettiness about her — rather a handsome, sun-tinged beauty, waiting to blossom into youthful fertility. Then he added: *idealized symbol of this country*.

Symbolic or not, it was himself that increasingly idealized her. Some Sunday afternoons, himself fishing with a rod and reel taken from stock, he spoke to her. Once he lay sprawled on the warm sand, and she came and knelt beside him. She asked what he was reading? He showed it was an anthology of new Australian poets. He read two poems to her. She said she liked them, though she didn't read much. But her sister had. Her sister once won a prize for an essay, and she'd written poems too. Of course, that was before she'd got married.

His conversations with Victoria on his nightly visits remained on the safe subjects of the shop, the coming and going of boats from the jetty, the catches of fish by people who came to the shop. Once, though, she asked what he intended to do after she left hospital. Then it all came spilling out in an unordered rush as he told of Bruthern and the theatre at Leeds and the television producer, of theatres in Hamburg and Hannover, in Passau and East Berlin, of his hiking in the mountains, of chance meetings with people in trains, of a couple met while sheltering from rain beneath a linden tree in a palace garden.

Amazed at his own hunger to tell, he kept telling until he ran himself out.

Then there was silence between them, until she asked:

'What happened to that ambition to build a uniquely Australian Culture?'

'That dream of a gum-tree culture!' he said. 'Pathetic! Pathetic and hopeless!'

'Not quite hopeless,' she said. 'There's that anthology of poems you loaned me, for instance.'

Just then the visitors bell rang and he escaped past three quite old women who watched a television set where a spangle-suited compere asked questions and gave away television sets.

That conversation, however, continued in his mind. He read local poets and story-writers, and some mornings put aside his work on Flaubert to write down scraps of conversations from people who came to the shop, descriptions of the bay and of boats and of fishing, of his girl from the beach.

Intruding among these notebook entries were others that read: June 2, *Antonius und Cleopatra* opens at the Gartentheatre, Hannover; June 10, *Marat Sade* at Berliner Ensemble; June 20, they're playing *Mutter Courage* at the Herrnhausen.

One day he told Victoria he had written to his former boss in Melbourne, asking if his old job was available. Victoria told him he should take wages for his work at the shop.

Soon after that he closed the shop at eleven one morning, took a taxi to the hospital and returned with Victoria to the flat. He opened the door on a table already set with a vase of poinsettias, cutlery, a bowl of salad; and he set to grilling steaks of mackeral and produced from the fridge a bottle of moselle. That night he slept on a canvas stretcher in a storeroom at the shop.

Some days later a neighbour drove her through rain to the shop. She came in through the doorway on her crutch. Half an hour later she asked why he'd replaced all the plastic reels with wooden ones? You can see the grain, he said. There's craftsmanship there. But they cost more, she said. You'd have sold four times the number in plastic ones. And whattabout the biros with dames that come starkers when you hold 'em up? Where're they? Sold 'em, he said. And didn't replace? But they sell! They're crap, he said. Bloody crap!

Then they were shouting at each other, shouting above the sound of rain on the iron roof of the shop. Abruptly, they stopped. Each sat at a distance from the other, each behind a different counter.

After a time, Victoria hopped on one leg to the deepfreeze. She took out two *Fruitos*, peeled the paper back from the ice of one, supported herself on counter tops as she carried it to him. Then they sat behind the one counter, each sucking on *Fruitos* and staring out at the rain.

That rain was driven in by a northerly that brought to an end the hot weather that had burned right through the months of Autumn and even the first month of Winter.

Rodney Hallens did not write the next morning. Instead he passed between evacuating campers, to the beach. The sea was at half-ebb, lying flat and innocently smooth; but high on the beach in a ragged line that margined the whole curving bay, the sea had thrown back, it seemed, all the wrack and rubbish of the bayside town. He walked beneath the threat of an indigo sky, kicking over bottles, dead bream, sodden newspapers, mackerel heads, red plastic buckets, green plastic ice-cream cans, tangled line, a dunny can encrusted with oysters. Gulls flashed white against the sky as they swooped to quarrel over dead fish.

Gulls picking among the rubbish of the town for what sustains them, he thought. Symbol of the artist?

Victoria thought so when he told her. She was

reading the morning paper.

'They're bringing all the troops home,' she said. 'To drum up votes for the next popularity poll.'

He said she was becoming as big a cynic as himself.

'You ought to be pleased,' she said. 'And there's rubbish here for you to pick among — that's your meat.'

It was not the gulls, though; it was the girl who became truly symbolic to him.

On his last Saturday at the Bay, Victoria and he ate at the restaurant next to the shop and he took her home, then walked alone to the pub. Under a canvas awning, a girl in plastic sombrero twanged and yodelled into a microphone with amplification turned to LOUD. Across bodies that swayed when they stood, tables littered with glasses, bottles, cigarette butts and potato crisp packets, he saw his girl from the beach. He mimed offer of a drink. She shook her head, but crossed to him to explain she was waiting to go home with her sister. There at the table to which she returned was the sister and her husband. In bright shirt and shorts, the husband was sitting on one chair with his fat legs propped on another. He could not have been more than thirty, but his stomach formed a mound from thigh to chest above which his face sat within a rolled collar of fat. He poured Coca-cola, then rum into his glass, then his wife's. She passively accepted as she tore at another packet of potato crisps with her teeth.

So this was what had become of the girl who once won a prize for an essay and who wrote poems before she was married.

Hallens watched as she crunched potato crisps and drank. Her youth, curiosity, and whatever had once stirred her to write essays and poems, now quite drowned in rum-and-Coke, rum-and-dry, rum-and-Fanta.

It was a tableau from that scene — with his girl

from the beach waiting, it seemed to him, to become like her sister — that occupied his mind through the two nights and a day of trains speeding south.

That image stayed with him through the southern Winter, through his driving to country towns, through conversations over samples and catalogues and order books and cups of coffee with customers he had farewelled almost a year before. That so much youthful beauty and verve might be traded for such obscene security, seemed to him a tragedy greater than Oedipus.

He shared a flat with his own younger sister, who railed at him for his detachment from politics since his return. Her life was very much as his own had been when he still counted himself among the faithful. Only occasionally did he accompany her to a meeting or walked with her on frost-tingling nights pushing pamphlets into letter boxes.

He finished his précis of episodes and completed the first script of *Sentimental Education*. He posted these to Bruthern, enclosing a letter to the English producer.

His own mail box brought him newspaper clippings of reviews of his play which was produced at Leeds without his presence at rehearsals. The play was accounted an artistic, though not commercial, success. An enclosed note informed him a statement of royalties and payment would follow.

It was some ten weeks before the money order arrived. When it did and he added it to what he had been able to save, he had more than sufficient for an economy class fare to London. Still, he lingered. One of his plays was being produced by an amateur group. From this he received no payment, though some acclaim. His sister was loud in her praise. Together with her bearded boyfriend-of-the-moment, she threw a party for him from which his bladder ached for days.

He worked at further episodes of *Sentimental Education*, though, increasingly, he found himself distracted by the work of young local poets. None of them individually great, but reaching an increasing audience with a collective voice of reassessment.

Taking their standpoint for his own, he again attempted what had always failed him: to capture in story a part of the mood and colour of the present time. The details were ready at hand, for these were to be taken from his own life; but the shape eluded him. Shape, he saw, was a matter of drawing limits; above all, the points of departure and resolution. Yet ending must be already present in beginnings. So he was frustrated from even beginning, for in this story of himself what could contain the resolution of the story's conflict while his own remained unresolved?

The English producer wrote that they could well be interested in his proposed series, but a great deal of consultation would be necessary before a final decision. When could they expect to see him.

Weeks later, Bruthern wrote:

> Old Cock
>
> You might get away with the stay-at-a-distance bit with plays, but that'll never work with TV. True, television producers think they're J.C. — but it's you that's got to produce the miracles. Miracles, Old Cock — on the spot!
>
> Are y' bloody coming or aren't you?
>
> Cheers and beers
>
> Michael B.

As he had with the producer's letter, he put off answering Bruthern's.

Four day's later, another letter arrived. This letter bore a Queensland postmark:

> Rod,
>
> Val wrote you've kept putting off making the decision whether or not to return to

London. Now that at last I have two good legs to stand on, I also have decisions to make. For months, the weather has been foul, resulting in the caravan park, the esplanade flats, and my till, all being quite empty.

One choice is to go begging to the bank for a loan. If that fills my begging bowl, I might last until the campers return at Xmas — and may yet make a go of it.

My other choice is presented by Mr Restaurant next door. He wants more room and has been badgering me to sell.

Should I have a bargain sale sell-up and return south?

If I'm able, I'll put off making my decision until I hear yours.

Love Vicki.

The implication in those last lines shouted to him as loudly as the demand for a decision from Bruthern's.

He was carrying both letters with him when he asked directions from his last customer of the day, then sped at a hundred and twenty over bitumen, scanning the roadside ahead for a sign.

He knew this to be his sign even before he read the words and the distance. He slowed, then turned along the indicated stony track towards high scattered gums. As he came nearer the hips and shoulders of rock ahead, the track became sandy, the gums low and crowded by banksia.

Ahead was a shallow ford and he took it at a run, but soon slipped into low gear when the path rose abruptly in deep red wheeltracks ahead. At first he skidded in wheeltracks and climbed, then the wheels slewed sideways and he could go no further.

He climbed the red sand track on foot, towards the buttress of rock that rose like a huge fist above the heath and the banksias and stringy-bark gums. Sweating and with cold air burning in his throat, he arrived at the rock. Beneath the knuckles of the rock was a long sheltering wall, its length of fourteen or more feet covered to head-height with rock paintings.

In daubs of rust-red ochre were life-sized drawings of hands and hands stencilled in ochre, then smaller and simpler finger-daubed figures hunting, climbing trees, throwing spears. There were lizard designs and figurative trees with down-sloping branches. Central were two figures standing together with hands touching.

A board placed by a country town historical society stated little was known of the people who made the paintings, but this was presumed to be a place of religious significance.

The day he had left Europe he had come from a place of another religion, the chapel where Leonardo had spread *The Last Supper* across an entire wall. This that he now stood before was plainly not the creation of a single towering giant, but the work of many unknown hands recording their life and place and times.

Yet if this was the sign he had come to take as his own, a thought came with a wry laugh chasing at its heels. Signs, he saw, were there wherever he chose to see them, and he could take his pick.

It was dark when he drove past the wheat silos, the saleyards, the supermarkets to the hotel where he was booked to stay.

Renovations had recently commenced, for above the door were pipes and planks of scaffolding. The licencee proudly announced he'd air-conditioned the place since he last stayed, then lowered his voice to say, actually, they were having a spot of trouble with the bloody thing.

He was too late for dinner at the hotel, so he ate at a nearby steak-and-chips cafe, before going to his room. There was only a bed, chair, wardrobe and chest of drawers. The room was hot and seemed airless. He strained to raise the window, until he saw the screw-heads that now held it sealed shut. He began taking off his clothes, emptying his pockets as he did. He took out Bruthern's letter and again read it. He re-read Victoria's letter. He placed both letters on top of the chest of drawers.

From his satchel he took an exercise book and pencils and tried to write by sitting on the chair with the exercise book on the drawers. Neither the writing nor the sitting worked: his knees against the drawer handles forced him to lean forward and up at an angle. Then he tried crouching on the seat. Then standing and stooping.

In the end, he placed the exercise book on the seat of the chair and knelt on the carpet's faded pattern. And he, kneeling, a ridiculous suppliant in socks and underpants, wrote:

For a one-time believer become estranged, the Church prescribes he kneel — then believe. A rational man, surely, would reverse the prescription, requiring decision first, then the deed; and insist the prescribed order reveals merely the suppliant's will. Yet by this illogic might an unsure painter draw his first charcoal strokes; by this tenet might a writer start a story . . .

Graham Sheil was born in Melbourne in 1938. His boyhood was split between Melbourne's outer eastern suburbs, and the goldmining country south of Ballarat where his father had both gold and diatomaceous earth mines. He left school at fifteen and began writing his first stories in the late 1960's.

His play, *Mad Like Lasseter* was performed at the Q Theatre, Adelaide, and at Goulburn's Southern Regional Theatre. Melbourne's New Theatre produced the plays *Work-a-Day* and *New Australians Rehearse the Workingman's Paradise*.

Two new plays, *This is the Way the World Ends* and *Bright Jewel for the Crown* will receive their premiers in Melbourne and Brisbane during 1987.

Graham Sheil lives with his family at Ringwood, Victoria; and together with his wife is proprietor of an optical importing and wholesaling company.

AUSTRALIAN SHORT STORIES

SUBSCRIPTIONS

4 issues of Australian Short Stories $15.00 posted in Australia. Posted overseas, surface mail $20.00. Makes cheques payable to Pascoe Publishing Pty. Ltd. and mail to P.O. Box 51, Fairfield 3078.

Back Copies: copies of Nos. 1-13 available for $3.00 ea. posted from the above address.

Name (please print) ....

Address ....

Bankcard/Visa: Please charge to my Bankcard ☐ Visa ☐

Card No. ....

Signature ....

Cheque, Money Order, Bankcard Authorization enclosed for $ ....

being for .... subscriptions and .... back copies

Please indicate your selection of issues

1983				1984				1985				1986			
1	2	3	4	5	6	7	8	9	10	11	12	13	14	15	16

PASCOE PUBLISHING